LESSONS FROM MY MOTHER'S LIFE

TAM MAY

Quotes in the text are as follows:

Epigraph

Friedan, Betty. *The Feminine Mystique (50th Anniversary Edition)*. W. W. Norton & Company, 2013 (original publication date: 1963). Kindle digital file.

"Mother of Mischief"

Epigraph

Barnes, Djuna. *Nightwood*. Harcourt, Brace, & Company, 2006 (original publication date: 1937). Kindle digital file.

Charlotte Anna Perkins Gilman quote:

From "The Housewife"

https://www.poetryfoundation.org/poems/46058/the-housewife-56d225d31d71a

To Aila and Becky for their confidence in me as a writer and their enthusiastic support of my work.

"A mother might tell her daughter, spell it out, 'Don't be just a housewife like me.' But that daughter, sensing that her mother was too frustrated to savor the love of her husband and children, might feel: 'I will succeed where my mother failed, I will fulfill myself as a woman,' and never read the lesson of her mother's life."

— Betty Friedan, *The Feminine Mystique*, p. 71

AUTHOR'S NOTE: THE LESSONS OF OUR MOTHERS' (AND OUR GRANDMOTHERS') LIVES

I'm including this author's note because if I didn't, this book would have some unfinished business.

Lessons From My Mother's Life is the second edition of my first book, *Gnarled Bones and Other Stories*, published in January 2017. This current edition went through a tremendous evolution in so many ways: style, tone, timeframe, themes, and purpose, to name a few. I felt I couldn't release it without including some kind of background for my readers.

When I published *Gnarled Bones and Other Stories*, I was at the beginning of my writing journey. At that time, I was engrossed with psychological fiction (fiction that explores the emotional reality of characters —Edith Wharton, Margaret Atwood, and Toni Morrison, for example), and I still am. I began where many writers begin — my own emotional experiences. The five stories that made up *Gnarled Bones* had been sitting in a folder on my computer for nearly fifteen years. When I wrote them, I was going through a rough time, and my perceptions of my family and my childhood were shifting. I was exploring my own psychological reality, some of which found its way into stories rather like beliefs that become part of your being without your really knowing it until something happens to challenge those beliefs.

I revised those original stories, organized them, and released them in *Gnarled Bones*. My goal was not only to give readers a deeper look at what we call "family dysfunction" laced with loss, fear, and guilt, but, on a more practical level, to "test the waters" as an author and discover my readers. I am one of those people who learns by doing, and I knew I could only read so many books on self-publishing before I had to jump in with both feet and pray I didn't make a total fool of myself.

The book received little attention, but the generous readers who did read and review it encouraged me. Many remarked that the stories were too short and their endings too abrupt. These were legitimate critiques and, over time, I understood why I left the stories half-finished. A writer might end a story prematurely when the characters are at the point of an emotional break-through, and the writer herself may be reluctant to dive into those difficult psychological moments the characters are experiencing in those breakthroughs. I realized this is exactly what I had done with the stories in *Gnarled Bones*. They told of people who, incited by unexpected incidents, see moments of their past they had been blind to and change their perceptions on life to move toward a more hopeful future. The characters in those stories were going through such moments in their lives, and I was afraid to take them through to the end. Additionally, a fellow writer who had read some of my other works remarked how my fiction offers something comforting, no matter what the subject matter. I realized in *Gnarled Bones* I had shortchanged readers of this gift. As a result, although I had meant the stories to point toward hope for the future, some readers found them too dark and depressing.

There was another reason I decided to release this second edition. I started out as many writers do, writing about my own time, or rather, an unidentified time period interpreted as "the present." In 2018, my writing went from contemporary to historical fiction. I wanted to take my lifelong passion for writing about women and write stories about women who defied the constraints of their time. I think history gets a bad rap because we're forced in school to memorize dates and events that represent the past and have no relationship to how we live in the present. We forget history isn't just about what happened, but who it happened to, how they felt, how they reacted, and how it changed the way future generations will feel and react. It's about the way people lived emotionally, their ideas, beliefs, and values and, most importantly, how we can see our own lives shaped in the shadow of the past. Historical events are the context in which people live, but they are not in and of themselves the reason why history is still relevant to us today. They are a path for us to trace back what used to be to understand what is now and what the possibilities are for the future.

In this way, historical fiction is ideal. A college professor of mine once said, "History is about what happened. Fiction is about what *should* have happened." In fiction, we reinterpret the past through the lens of what we know and understand about ourselves today. We enjoy reading about people, events, and emotions of the past, certainly, but in fiction, we can take them into our own lives and relate to them in a different and more meaningful way.

In 2019, I already knew I wanted to create a new edition of *Gnarled Bones* which included placing the collection in the past. As with many historical fiction writers, I have certain eras I'm drawn to, such as the Gilded Age (the last quarter of the 19th century) and the Progressive Era (the first few decades of the 20th century). But when I started to reimagine *Gnarled Bones*, I found neither of these really fit. The stories in that collection were about complex psychological issues that I felt belonged to a later era. So I struggled to decide what time period would be the most emotionally relevant to the new edition.

The answer came to me when I reread one of the first editorial reviews I ever received. The reviewer remarked the style and tone of the stories reminded him of the 1950s, so much so that he expected housewives to walk around with curlers in their hair (this is a paraphrase, not a direct quote). That comment was my "a-ha!" moment, and it hit me why the fiction in *Gnarled Bones* were so complex. Many of the stories in that first edition were about women trying to define themselves as women beyond the expectations of feminine behaviors, values, and stereotypes. I recalled reading an excerpt from Betty Friedan's seminal book *The Feminine Mystique* in a course I took during graduate school. Published in 1963, Friedan traces her quest for the "happy housewife" after her experiences as a journalist interviewing women in the 1950s for magazine articles. Her journey led her to identify what she calls "The Problem That Has No Name."

What was this problem? Simply, that American women in the 1950s, specifically, middle-class white housewives (let's establish right off that Friedan was talking about a very specific sector of American life) had everything any woman could ever want at that time — faithful and prosperous husbands, plenty of money, smart kids, a nice house in the suburbs, a nice car or two, and, in the post-war boom, a whole lot of nice things. They didn't have to go out and work for their living; they didn't have to struggle and suffer, and they didn't have to figure out who they were as individuals because they were defined by their relationships (wife, mother, daughter, caretaker, etc.) They even had a college degree to show they weren't just pretty paper dolls wearing aprons and baking cookies. They had everything, and yet, they were discontented, despaired, and unfulfilled. Hence, as Friedan saw it, they had a problem that didn't, at that time, have a name.

Friedan was so interested in this reoccurring theme in the lives of women she encountered that she embarked on a quest to find out why they were unhappy. The answer she came up with "the feminine mystique." This isn't just about women who fulfill their feminine duties by devoting their lives to their husbands, families, children, and church. It isn't just about the idea that this is what all women should aspire to be, but that this is what *should* make them happy. Friedan's 593-page book argues that the feminine mystique was a bill of goods sold to women by institutions (most of them controlled by men) in the 1950s and early 1960s, some of which included women's magazines, the medical and psychiatric establishments, and ad agencies.

I realized many of the stories in *Gnarled Bones*, re-set in the 1950s and early 1960s would mirror the feminine mystique and its discontentments in ways even women today could understand and identify with. The original collection was loosely tied together by themes of loss, fear, and guilt. I wanted this edition to be grounded in a historical context particularly relevant to women socially and psychologically.

This is *not* to say that women are still struggling and oppressed in the 21st century in the same ways they were in the post-war era. We've come a very long way, and we can be proud to watch our daughters and granddaughters pursue their dreams and juggle family, work, hobbies, and anything else they want to do in life. This is also not to say the post-war eras didn't have their heroines and warrior women. The women who broke out of the feminine mystique during these decades are plentiful, and the topic for another book in the future. But the general feeling of discontentment among women did prevail (as many women still living from that era can attest) and it's a sentiment worthy of exploration in fiction.

As for this edition of my first book, now retitled *Lessons From My Mother's Life*, three of the stories are set in the 1950s and two in the early 1960s. These are the years when the feminine mystique was at its peak, before the birth of the second-wave feminist movement that grew from, among other works, Friedan's book. The protagonists in these stories are women at different stages of their lives, from the young and eager bride-to-be to the mother experiencing the turbulent emotions of the empty nest. The thread tying these women together is their realization that the feminine mystique, that bill of goods they were sold about what would fulfill them as women, is, in fact, not enough for them.

Some readers have said that the stories are still dark and depressing. The purpose of these stories is not to give a happily-ever-after ending (because they question the reality of the happily-ever-after ending that put women in a box in the 1950s). But each woman in the five stories is moving toward a new realization of her worth and what is left off the page is the new directions their lives will take which will be, in a sense, their own individual happily-ever-after.

As with all my other books, the setting for most of these stories is the San Francisco Bay Area (although the Los Angeles area plays a cameo role in "Soul Destinations"). I once wrote a guest blog post about how San Francisco became a symbol of autonomy and freedom for me when I first lived there in 1995. It became my first home away from home where I found myself as a woman and a writer. It felt like the logical place for my protagonists to find themselves also.

As I reviewed the stories from the original collection, I realized not all of them would fit in with my intention for this collection. "Bracelets," for example, was more about the loss of childhood innocence, and I couldn't make it fit thematically in this new edition. I removed that story and included "Two Sides of Life" instead. I changed the title of two of the stories because I felt the new titles would better suit the characters' psychological journeys. So "A First Saturday Outing" became "Fumbling Toward Freedom," and "Broken Bows" became "Soul Destinations." A fourth story remained from the original edition ("Mother of Mischief") and has been considerably expanded, its ending now complete and, I hope, more satisfying and uplifting than the one in the first edition.

I think the biggest change I made was to remove the title story of the first book. In that first edition, the story "Gnarled Bones" was, I felt, the apex of the collection, encompassing those themes of loss, fear, and guilt that held the five stories in that version together. It made sense to me to title the book after that story. I tried reworking it for this new edition, but in doing so, I realized the themes involved (loss and guilt, and, further, the way in which the horrors of Nazism affected the third generation) simply did not fit the themes in this new edition. I also realized the story could and should be its own full-length novella. I replaced that story here with "Devoted," and I might publish *Gnarled Bones* as a stand-alone historical novella sometime in the future.

This second edition includes five stories, all full-length, in addition to a bonus excerpt from *The Specter*, the first book of my Waxwood Series (a historical women's fiction coming-of-age series set in the last decade of the 19th century).

I hope readers who have read the first edition will be very pleased with the changes here, and I hope they will agree the stories are more complete, less melancholic, and more thoughtful and enjoyable. I also hope readers will find themselves or their mothers or grandmothers in these characters and understand what some women might have gone through in this era. Most importantly, I hope that readers will see their own resilience reflected in these characters and their lives, no matter what their age or background.

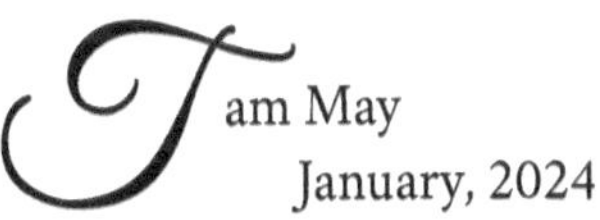

Tam May
January, 2024

FUMBLING TOWARD FREEDOM

Want more feisty heroines who go against conventions? Love intricate mysteries with humor and a fun cast of characters? Then you'll love my free offer at the end of this book! So don't forget to check that out when you get to the end. Happy reading!

The tiny flat Susan found for them had a view of Golden Gate Park. She stood on the fire escape and traced the grid-like streets, following Ninth Avenue down until it spilled right into the park. She could just see the arches of the Japanese Tea Garden and the straight line of cars that would curve around the lake where the ducks bobbed like pinecones on the surface of the cobalt water.

But she barely had time to enjoy the view now. For the last three days, she had been cleaning the place, arranging and rearranging the second-hand furniture, and shopping for towels and dishes and all the other essentials. Pete chided her, insisting, "You should register at Macy's so people can buy that stuff as wedding presents, and we don't have to spend a dime." But in two weeks, this would be their first home together, and she wanted the the little place to have something. She had given in to his insistence that they wait until they had more money to buy a new couch and bed and the rocker she had always wanted. He snorted about "the whims of impossible brides" but she had gotten her way.

The last of the kitchen cupboards were completed that Friday evening, and as she waited for Pete to come from UCSF to take her to dinner, she lingered near the fire escape, her hand on the handle of the sliding glass door. But something about going out there and becoming part of Judah and Irving's quiet streets in the growing darkness unnerved her. When they were married and she was no longer alone, they could watch the starry night together. Without Pete, it felt wrong.

She wandered into the living room, peering out the window to watch for his bright blue Ford. She knew the street well, as she and Pete had walked it many times when she came to the city to visit him. Even in the dull evening light, the street was familiar, but the flat still felt like a foreign country. Unlike her parents' sprawling colonial house in Lester, the walls here were knitted close, the only bedroom tight with the little furnishings they bought for it, and the kitchen overflowed with the pots and pans her mother had given her.

"You must start experimenting, dear," Mom had said in her chiding way. "You haven't much time before the wedding to perfect your cooking. Pete will expect a good meal every night when he comes home from work."

Warmth filled her chest. In two weeks, they would be free, she and Pete. They had even gotten the idea of an early marriage past her parents.

"Best to wait until Pete is out of school," her father had advised the night she told them.

"But he won't be in school," she insisted. "He'll be interning at St. Mary's after the summer."

"What does a doctor's internship pay?" her father scoffed. "Peanuts!"

"It's expensive to live in the city," her mother reminded her.

"We've arranged all that," she said. "Pete's father is going to help us. He says he can afford to give us enough. With Pete's salary, we can pay our bills and not starve. He's even going to give Pete the Ford he's had his eye on so we'll have a car."

"That's all well and good," said her father. "You know we like Pete and his family. They're decent people. But even decent young men get in over their heads when they have responsibilities. Young men are three times more likely to go into debt with a wife than without one."

"You read that in the paper." Her mother laughed. "You know how they're always exaggerating those studies."

"And when the first baby comes?" He gave her an inquisitive look.

"That won't be for a while." She played with the spoon on her dessert plate.

"It might be sooner than you think!"

"Another cup of coffee, Mike?" Her mother shoved the pot toward him.

"All I'm saying," he grumbled, "is you and Pete shouldn't do anything rash. Your mother and I waited two years after we got engaged before the wedding. Mr. Tuttle promised me a promotion at the plant, and we timed it very carefully."

"Oh, Dad, love isn't about calculations." Susan smiled. "It's about sticking together, no matter the odds."

He held up his hand. "Don't quote the wisdom of Lydia the Love Expert to me. That might work for the editors of *Seventeen* or whatever you girls read, but not for me."

"I don't read *Seventeen* anymore and you know it." She laughed and threw an orange at him, which he caught with a perfect backhand and began to peel.

That night, when she was getting ready for bed, her mother

had come into her room. She was playing Doris Day on the portable phonograph, and the galloping tune filled the room, making the pink and white trimmings brighter and the flowers on the wallpaper look as if they were ready to bloom.

Her mother sat on the bed, fingering the Bambi stuffed toy sitting on the shelf above. "Pretty song," she murmured.

"From your namesake, Mom." Susan shut off the record player. Somehow, the song that began with a rogue follower and ended with marriage did not delight her that evening. "I suppose you're going to tell me Dad is right, and I should speak to Pete about postponing the wedding."

"I wasn't going to say that."

"Why not? "Susan challenged. "You're always saying I should listen to Dad because he's usually right." She laid out her pajama pants and top on the bed.

"He almost always is." Then, in a wispy voice, she asked, "What about your studies, dear?"

"I never wanted to go to college anyway," Susan said. "If you and Dad hadn't insisted —"

"All your friends were going," her mother argued. "We didn't want you to feel left out."

"Lots of girls leave college to get married," Susan pointed out. "They don't feel left out."

"I know, but college is an experience every girl should have." Her mother rubbed Bambi's ear. "And, anyway, home economics won't exactly be useless to you in the future."

"I would rather learn on the job." She grinned. "The housewife job, that is. Like you did."

"Still," said her mother. "I think you should at least finish the three years you have left before you marry Pete."

Susan buttoned up the pajama top. "Would you have waited three years for Dad?"

Her mother's gaze faded. "That was different. There was a

depression, and two people had a better chance than one, especially if one of those was a woman."

Susan stiffened with the stubborn determination that had gotten her into trouble more than once as a child. "Well, I want to give Pete his chance to be a fine doctor by giving him a home."

"You told me you enjoy your classes," her mother pointed out. "Especially Anthropology."

"Oh, they're interesting enough," Susan said. "I like to learn about the things people left behind in ancient times. But I would never *do* anything with it."

"And your sorority sisters," her mother murmured. "You like them."

"Mom, half of them are going to get married before their senior year," Susan laughed. "So you see, you don't have to be afraid of my being left out. It's the ones who finish that will be left out."

"You might regret it later," her mother ventured.

"I'll never regret marrying Pete." She put the record away and shut the lid on the phonograph.

"That wasn't what I meant."

"Did you regret it?" Susan asked.

"I told you, it was a different time."

"Well, if you were me, right now, would you make the same choice now as you did then?" Susan peered at her.

Her mother didn't answer. She began to attend to the bed, removing the pink coverlet, folding back the blanket, puffing up the pillows. She watched as Susan climbed in, then set Bambi back in his place on the shelf.

Only when her hand was on the light switch did Susan hear her say, "I don't think I would. No, I don't think I would."

~~~~~

Her mother's parting words that night seared into her like a brand on a cow's hide. For months afterward, the words *I don't think I would* haunted her at night like Bambi's huge glass eyes.
~~~~~

They slipped from the tongues of her sorority sisters as they chattered at breakfast, squeaked from the chalk on the blackboards during lectures, and screamed out at her from her textbooks. She was glad when the school year was over and she could pack for San Francisco to find her and Pete the flat.

The day before she was to leave, Pete managed to come down to Lester to iron out the last details of her apartment search. They sat on the porch where the summer flies had already discovered the rhododendrons and the lavender. The heavy perfume floated into the warm evening mist. Even with Pete's arm around her shoulders and the calm night sifting through the bright pink and purple flowers, she felt restless.

"Don't fret, honey," Pete said in that lazy tone of his. "You'll find a place just right for us."

"It isn't that." She brushed her finger against the rough arm of the wicker couch. "I was thinking of my mother."

He chuckled. "I suppose a girl always thinks of her mother when she's about to get married." He kissed her cheek.

She turned to him. "Petey, do you suppose I ought to go on with my studies, at least for a while?"

"You mean after we're married?" He shrugged. "Don't tell me *that's* what's been eating away at you."

"I suppose I could always take courses at the City College," she ventured. "That wouldn't be too much."

"I thought you told me taking care of a home was a full-time job and a half."

"It is, but it doesn't need to be," she said. "It is for Mom, I mean. But there's so much to make it easier these days —"

"If that were really true, you wouldn't be going to college to learn homemaking, would you?" He nuzzled her cheek. "Don't worry, honey, you'll be busy. A doctor's wife has about all the work she can stand just being a doctor's wife."

"I just don't want to not go to college and wish ten years from now that I had." She leaned back, staring at a gecko crawling up the balcony pole in the glow of the porch lights.

"Well, if that's what's worrying you, you can always go back," he insisted. "When the kids are grown, of course."

She rose and made her way to the rhododendron, touching the delicate pink petals. "I won't go back. I know I won't."

"How can you know a thing like that?" he asked with a boyish sniff. "Women's intuition is a fallacy. It's been proven in scientific studies."

"I'm not talking about science!" She glanced at him over her shoulder.

"Don't be a sap, honey." He yawned loudly behind her. "We should turn in. I want to get an early start for the drive tomorrow."

"It just seems like a waste — such a waste —" she murmured as Pete led her inside the house.

Sleep turned out to be the tonic she needed, for when Pete woke her with the darkness outside still lashing at the windows, her apprehension from the night before had lifted. She could be cheerful as they drove the Ford onto the highway, discussing where they might go on their honeymoon if Pete could get the time off.

Now in the apartment, her mind raced, but she couldn't remember the places Pete mentioned. She only remembered they struck her as the sort of places a young doctor and his wife would go on their honeymoon.

"Pete's so cultured," she mused as she returned to the living room and looked out the window for the Ford's yellow lights. "He'll teach me to be cultured too."

Pete arrived only a little while later. She was already halfway down the stairs when he appeared, lugging his doctor's bag, his stethoscope swinging from his neck. She threw herself into his arms.

He laughed. "Get the things unpacked?"

"Not everything," she admitted. "But it's looking like home already."

Pete agreed as she led him around the apartment by the hand, pointing to what she had done and explaining why she had done it. He smiled. "I like how you always have a reason for what you do." He put an arm around her. "Not like other girls, who just go by their whims."

He insisted she dress up. "A fellow at school told me about the Villa Romana. He said they have great Italian food and a swank atmosphere."

She wore the cherry red dress with the square neckline that made her look like Snow White with her alabaster skin and dark brown hair, and dabbed herself with only the sheerest sheen of make-up, the way he liked. They strolled down the hill of Ninth Street, passing by the block apartment houses meshed with Victorian relics, all pressed together as if daring the next earthquake to rob them of their foundations.

They reached Irving and met with a wave of young people bouncing around on a Friday night, exploring the restaurants and bars with the eagerness of cows let out to pasture. The UCSF campus was not far off, so they met several of Pete's acquaintances, most of them young medical students, and a few of his professors with their wives. She felt a little dizzy from all the introductions, as she never was good with names, but the idea that she would soon belong with them gave her a warm calm feeling, as if someone had lit a candle inside of her.

When they reached the restaurant, she was relieved to see it had a subtle tone, unlike some of the places Pete had taken her to in the city where jazz bands blasted through intimate conversations. The rustic atmosphere gave way to the rumble of chatter around them. She let Pete order, glancing around with a smile. "Some of these people might be our neighbors," she said with a laugh.

"Oh, I don't know," said Pete. "Lots of people come here from all around the city. It's a big city, Sue."

"I'm not afraid of the big city," she declared with her stubbornness.

He laughed as the waiter set the wine in front of them. "Shall I make a toast?"

"Why not?"

He raised his glass. "To us, soon to be the little couple on top of the wedding cake."

She giggled, but as she drank down the sweet wine, she couldn't help but picture the cake topper with the tall T-shaped groom holding the arm of the bride in her quilted wedding dress and pink bouquet, both of them with bright smiles and glassy stares. The wine burned a little in her throat.

Over veal parmesan, they talked about the sites they would take in now that they had a whole weekend together. As usual, Pete seemed to know exactly what he wanted. "The Botanical Garden is right down the street," he said, pointing toward the window. "So is the Japanese Tea Garden."

"I didn't realize you were so fond of flowers." She squeezed lemon into her water glass. "Once we have the money, we'll have to buy a house with a large garden."

"It's the way they organized the gardens that interests me," said Pete. "And we'll see the Civic Center, of course."

"Of course," she echoed. "But I want to do cultural things too."

He laughed, nearly choking on his wine. "What ideas!"

"Why not?" She stiffened. "The girls in my sorority told me about a few places."

"How about the curio shops down in Chinatown?" There was a sparkle in his eye. "That's culture, isn't it?"

"I meant museums," she insisted. "Art, things like that."

"I thought they bored you."

"They bore *you*."

He was quiet as the waiter cleared their table and brought

the coffee. The chatter around them seemed to have increased as a large party had entered, creating a ribbon of shouts and laughter around them. "I suppose we might take in the de Young Museum," Pete said, raising his voice. "That's in the park too."

She looked down. "I was thinking —"

"What?" He leaned forward.

"I was thinking." She spoke louder. "The girls told me about an exhibition of Deenie Brown sculptures that's showing right now."

"Who's Deenie Brown?"

"A former sorority sister." Susan gnawed at her fingernail.

"Oh." His voice sounded metallic against the rising scrape of tables and chairs as the waiters scrambled to accommodate the large party.

"She only started doing showings last year, but the girls said she's made quite a splash in the Bay Area," Susan shouted over the noise.

"An amateur then," Pete said.

"She's very good, I'm told," said Susan. "And the exhibition is in the Erudition House."

"Strange name for an art gallery," Pete mused as he accepted the check the waiter put on their table.

"It's really some kind of old building," said Susan. "An old saloon or something."

"Oh." Pete gathered their coats. "Let's get out of here, honey. Too noisy to talk."

They went out into the warm night air. The street was less crowded than it had been, though there were still people about, walking slowly and enjoying the sweet, summer breeze.

She took Pete's arm. "You ought to take up tennis again, dear."

"Why, am I getting flabby?" He glanced down at his stomach.

"'Course not." She gave him a kiss on the nose. "I just know doctors like to be fit."

"I won't be a full-fledged doctor for a while," he said, grinning. "I don't think I have anything to worry about yet."

They walked in silence for a time, heaving a little at the incline as they made their way to the flat. "Let's take in the Gardens tomorrow. Botanical and Japanese." He gave a little laugh.

"What about the Deenie Brown exhibition?" She looked at him with pleading eyes.

"I don't even know where the Erudition House is," he grumbled. "Is it anywhere near the Cliff House?"

"No, silly," she said. "Down by Ocean Beach."

"That's far off, Sue," he said.

"Only the other side of the park," she pointed out.

She could see under the yellow light of the apartment house that he was annoyed. His left eyebrow curved a little toward the bridge of his nose and his lip set into a tight line. He didn't like it when she argued with him.

"Please, honey," she said. "The way the girls talked about it made it sound so interesting." She rubbed his arm.

He fished the car keys out of his pocket. "All right. Never let it be said I don't indulge my little lady's caprices of culture."

She threw her arms around his neck. She heard him mumbling as he retreated to his car, "Erudition! What kinda name is that anyway?"

~~~~~

The next morning, Susan woke up to a tentative fog lingering outside the bedroom window. By the time Pete came to get her from his shared flat near the campus, the fog had cleared to blue skies, and the promise of a blistering heat filtered through the screen. She dressed carefully in a peach and white polka-dot suit and straw hat.

"Our first outing," she murmured, smiling at Pete.

"Our first Saturday outing," he corrected. He had slipped on a
~~~~~

light gray jacket and taking up his Stetson hat, looking less stern than he did in his doctor's coat and stethoscope.

The city wind seemed equally willing to contribute to the pleasantness of the day, rolling sweetly against her lips like one of Pete's kisses. He drove the Ford carefully down Lincoln Way as she opened the window and stared in wonder at the richness of the shrubbery and trees along Golden Gate Park. As they turned onto the Great Highway facing the beach, her eyes feasted on the blank canvas of sky in front of them and the peak of blue-green waves in the distance.

"At least we have a nice view," Pete commented. "I'll bet you're glad to see the water after Lester."

"I once read that a new view means new prospects," she breathed.

He laughed. "A false prophet in one of your lady's magazines, no doubt."

"No, it's true, Petey," she said. "Don't you think it's true?"

"If you do, dear." She attributed the mechanical tone to his concentration on the road.

The museum was hidden among vegetation beyond the park's Dutch windmill. "Looks like your sorority sisters were right about the old building," Pete remarked, looking around with a note of distaste.

Susan felt as if they had been transported into the one-room schoolhouse. Tiny wooden desks were pushed up to the front of the room, where a blackboard against the wall showed the shadow of verb conjugations from a lost lesson. The windows were small and boxy but the glare shone bright through their polished glass.

"Of course!" she murmured. "Erudition. That means learning, doesn't it?"

Pete squinted through the glaring light. "I can't imagine any kid learning much in this foxhole."

A man in a loose-fitting suit approached them with a wide

smile and handed them a leaflet. "Welcome, folks. I see you're taken in by our artistic rendition of Matilda's Schoolhouse."

Pete gave him a blank stare. "I beg your pardon?"

"My great-grandma built this place as a little ol' schoolhouse in the last century." The man grew nostalgic. "Her name was Matilda, and she thought every child should have an education, no matter what. So she taught everyone who came through the door — even some grown-ups!" He laughed. "We turned it into a little ole place for art and culture, the wife and I."

"Interesting," mumbled Pete.

"Well, just take your time, folks, no hurry." The man stepped aside.

Susan's eyes felt as if they were stretched to the limit. Never had she seen such large sculptures, almost the size of Lotta's Fountain on Market Street. Or perhaps they just seemed gigantic in that small schoolhouse. Their brass finish made little marks on the walls where the sunlight hit them. These natural spotlights called to her, drawing her attention to so many different places that her head began to ache.

"Must you do that, dear?" Susan glanced at her fiancé. Pete had begun prying loose the knot on his tie.

"I just feel, I don't know, antsy in here. Like when I have to go to the morgue and look at a dead body."

Susan wrinkled her nose. "I told you this morning you could have left the tie at the flat. This is Saturday, after all."

"It's not the tie," he said. "This place sort of reminds me of times I went to my mother's classroom at the school and watched her teach. They stuck her in a little room near a closet, and with all those kids packed inside — "

"You felt stifled, you poor thing," she said in that kindly voice her mother used to speak to her father when he'd had a bad day.

"I can't imagine what it was like for those kids a hundred years ago," he lamented. "All these little windows. Why, you can hardly get air through them even with the ocean at your back."

Then, in a softer tone, he added, "My mom was always in that schoolroom." Suddenly, he tightened his hand in hers. "Oh, let's get this over with!" He began to walk quickly through the room.

Susan's breath came out in a gasp. "Wait a minute!"

He stopped, looking at her.

"I thought we could go through them one by one," she said. "You know, sort of take each one in on its own."

He leaned on one foot. "Have you ever been to an art exhibit before, Sue?"

"No, that's what I mean," she said, feeling her irritation rising. "That's why I want to go through it slowly."

"An exhibition is supposed to be viewed as whole, not each piece individually," he said. "And, anyway, I thought we agreed we would just be here for five minutes and then go on to the Park."

"What's the use of seeing an exhibition if we don't really see it?" she asked in her stubborn way.

"Well, I can't stand this suffocating place. I'll wait for you outside. Where there are proper benches." He said the last with a resentful glare toward the small desks.

"Oh, don't get mad!"

"I'm not," he insisted, though the flush in his face showed otherwise. "I would just rather spend our time on sights that are really worth seeing."

"The Botanical and Japanese gardens?" she asked in a rueful tone.

He grasped both her hands. "Sue, you're not going to be one of those wives who cultivates a whole bunch of weird interests, are you?"

"You mean interests apart from her husband's?" She looked away.

"It's fine to want art and culture now and then, but you've got to be sensible in the long run."

"I'm sure you'll teach me how to be more sensible." She patted his cheek. "But let me have my weird interests a little while longer."

He laughed and kissed her cheek. "All right, I'll come with you, but we'll see it just once."

They went around the room without lingering. To Susan, the brilliance of the sculptures seemed to challenge the sun, forcing it inside a patch of clouds. Pete's stride was wider than hers, making her feel as though she were passing through a revolving door, getting only a flash at the world beyond the spinning glass. And yet, the women in the sculptures made an impression in her mind of something important. She caught glimpses of their eyes, their teeth, their shoulders. She wanted to stop and examine them closely.

When they returned to the front of the room, Pete gave a loud sigh. "Now that's over with."

"We didn't see a thing, Petey," she said.

"I think we saw enough, don't you?"

Her stubborn streak made her lips stiff. "No, I don't. I told you, I want to study them properly." In a softer tone, she said, "Their eyes —"

"Whose eyes?"

"The women's, of course," she said. "They're trying to say something. Maybe if I can study them, I can figure out what it is."

He stared at her. "You're daffy."

"I didn't think you would understand," she murmured.

He glanced at his watch. "Well, all right, I'll give you ten minutes, and then we go on to the Botanical Garden."

"You're not coming with me?"

"I can't stand being in this room anymore. I'll wait for you outside." He lifted her chin gently in his hand. "Okay?"

"Okay." She smiled.

The moment he left, she felt immediately drawn to the women's eyes — immense eyes staring through her while at the same time trying to suck her into their plight, not for the sake of sympathy, but to bear witness to their misery.

As Susan dallied over the first two sculptures, her attention taken up by their detail, she began to see the sculptures were telling a story. All the women etched in brass were the same woman with the same waist-length hair bouncing down her shoulders and the same button nose and strong chin. At the third one, she knelt a little, staring at it, eye to eye.

She heard a voice behind her. "Go ahead and get up close. She's not going to bite you."

Susan turned and met the gaze of a woman who looked to be in her thirties. She was dressed like the beatniks Susan had seen in the movies — the tight-fitting turtleneck sweater, ranch pants, flats and a long necklace with a disk that swung like a pendulum around her slim neck.

Susan straightened with a nervous laugh. "I'm not so sure!"

"I am," she said as she held out her hand. "I'm Deenie Brown, and I made her."

"Oh!" Susan dropped the gloves she had been holding and swooped down to retrieve them, pulling herself together as she shook the woman's hand.

"Typical posh name, isn't it?" She grimaced. "Of course, my parents called me Wilhemina. Terrible, isn't it?"

"I think Wilhemina is a lovely name," Susan said. "I would name my daughter that, if I had one."

"You mean *when* you have one." The woman raised one eye sharply as the other remained steady.

Susan blushed and fiddled with her gloves.

"Her name is Circe." Deenie leaned one hand against the wall.

"I know who Circe is," Susan said.

"You know the legend, I'm sure." Her voice grated the thin schoolroom air. "What they teach in college. You're a college girl, aren't you?" Susan nodded. "This exhibition is about the fall of Circe."

"I didn't know she had a fall," said Susan. "I thought it was Odysseus who fell."

"Come." The woman took her arm. "I'll give you the guided tour. You look so bewildered, it's the least I can do. But we have to begin at the beginning."

They returned to the first sculpture, and Deenie's voice rose and fell like a storyteller. "Each sculpture represents a deeper crisis than the previous one, you see. That's the real story of Circe."

"The real story," Susan echoed.

"She was a wild woman when she was young. You see that here." She pointed to the first sculpture, where, indeed, a child posed among rocks and trees, bending down to a circle of daisies.

"She looks like the devil's child," Susan remarked. Turning red, she mumbled, "I didn't mean that."

Deenie laughed. "That's exactly how I pictured her. Lilith's child." Her voice rose. "No one could control Circe then."

"Maybe they didn't try," Susan ventured.

The woman gave her a sharp glance. "Oh, they tried, child. Believe me, they tried." She strolled on, explaining, "Here, she becomes an adolescent, but she still holds her own among the creatures in the mountains. She befriends a mountain lion."

Susan stared at the sculpture where the girl was now almost a woman, her hand on a cougar's head while the creature stared intensely at her. She shrank back a little.

"Then, she discovers a man in the woods," Deenie continued as they walked on. "A rather gallant man, a demigod, really. Not Hercules, but he looks rather like he could be his younger brother, don't you think?" She waited until Susan cast her eyes on the statue in front of her where a man with a well-defined torso lay on the ground with Circe standing over him.

"Did she fall in love with him?" Susan asked.

Deenie gave her the glance of the one-eyed cat. "She did indeed. Hence, her downfall."

Susan stiffened. "Oh, I don't think a woman falls down when she falls in love. On the contrary, she rises up."

The eye was amused. "That young man is your husband, I take it?"

"Fiancé," said Susan with a modest glance toward the doorway, where she could see Pete sprawled on one of the wooden benches.

"I should have realized," Deenie murmured. They reached the back of the room now where the desks sat askew across the floor. She turned to Susan and asked, "Well, what do you think of my lady Circe so far?"

Susan considered this for a moment. "It's like each face of hers in the sculptures absorbs the look of the one before."

Deenie was clearly pleased, as her patronizing gaze relaxed, making her almost pretty. "My intent was that each one would add something to the story, making it more complex than the last. A jaw leaping forward, a lip sagging with lost faith." Deenie swept her arm up. "And eyes revealing the consequence of one woman's entrapment."

"Oh, no," Susan objected. "She looks very happy."

"What a refreshing innocence you have." The woman's lips pierced like the edge of a knife.

"You're mocking me," Susan snapped.

"I take you very seriously." She took her arm again. "Come, child. I'm anxious to hear what you think of the rest of my Circes."

As they went down the other side of the room, Susan began to feel uneasy. She saw what Deenie meant by entrapment. Circe's face grew haggard even as her smile deepened with each sculpture. The bold thrust that had made the brass figures so tall and regal sank lower and lower, as if Circe were forced to crouch and crawl. As her body grew smaller, her eyes grew bigger.

"Why does she become smaller?" she ventured.

Deenie murmured, "She caught her demigod, you see."

Susan glared at her. "You're trying to imply he seduced her."

The artist smiled. "Seduction has no lasting effects, child, if the woman is willing. It's over and done with. It's being ensnared in a love without boundaries that does her in."

"You're confusing me," Susan confessed.

Deenie cast the cat eye toward the doorway. "I don't blame you for being confused. Everything can become a cage for a woman as young as yourself."

"Everything?" Susan echoed.

"Everything," she said. "Love. Marriage. Education. Work. Art. You have to choose one way or another like Circe." She cast her eye on the last sculpture. "That's the real hellfire and damnation of a woman's life. You're always forced to choose."

Susan felt her neck stiffen and her eyes grow cold. She realized she didn't want to look at the brass figure. She suddenly became terrified by a feeling of something trying to sweep her up into its arms like a menacing ghost. Deenie looked at her for a few minutes and then, in silence, stepped back and leaned against the back wall.

The last sculpture was a tiny Circe, the figure standing on the large brass pedestal no bigger than a paperweight. It was, in fact, not a figure at all, but a face made up of eyes. A box with gold rings closed around the face, making the eyes squeeze through the bars. They were snaring eyes, crooked and grasping like hands, as if they wanted to reach out for help.

A scream racked Susan's body. She shut her eyes tightly as her father had taught her to do when she was a child, awakened in the middle of the night by a frightening dream. How reassuring to squeeze the monster out of her mind just by shutting her eyes! As she opened them, she saw a space untouched by anything so cruel as a bloated monster or clawing eyes. A couple passed through the door and gave her the vague smile of strangers.

She turned to Deenie, though she could hardly see her face in the shadow between the wall and the door. "What's the name of this exhibition?"

She heard the answer. *"Fumbling Toward Freedom."*

"She did the right thing," Susan murmured. "She *must* have done the right thing!"

She ran out of the museum. Pete jumped up and caught her shoulders. She felt her shoes scraping against the red bricks.

"Honey, are you all right?"

She looked at him, her head spinning. "Of course I'm all right!"

"You look as if someone twenty years dead just grabbed her hand."

She let out a high giggle. "Circe tried to claw my face with her eyes."

"Who?"

"The woman trapped in the sculptures," she said.

"Here, Sue, you'd better sit down for a minute." He led her to the bench. "Let me see if I can get you a glass of water."

"I told you, I'm all right," she insisted.

"It's that room," he said. "Why they decided to open a museum here is beyond me. Well, don't worry, honey, we're going to some spacious gardens now."

"Gardens," she murmured. "Yes. Flowers, orchids, wedding blossoms. Oh, she did the right thing!"

"I should never have agreed to this whim," Pete lamented. "I should have known it would upset you. These beatniks, they don't even live on the same planet as us!"

"What planet would that be?" she asked, her voice harsh. "A safe and sane planet? But how can one be safe and sane in a cage?"

"Really, Sue, you do have a morbid imagination sometimes." He kissed her. "We'll have to work on that."

"So many things you'll have to work on about me," said Susan. "That's what you're planning, isn't it?"

He fumbled for the car keys, "A doctor helps people with what ails them, doesn't he?"

Her head had stopped spinning. She could see clearly the way the sun made the blue sky bright and metallic, the rolling line of the ocean across the street, and the long black road that stretched toward the park. "But you'll be my husband, not my doctor!"

He gave her a tolerant look. "Come on, honey. We'll take in the Botanical Garden, and then go for a nice, quiet lunch."

"Are husbands supposed to fix wives?" Her voice grew shrill. "Like a toy-maker fixes dolls?"

"Sue, really." He sniffed. "I don't know what that beatnik said to you, but their babble can make anybody think they're crazy. I've seen 'em in the cafe near the university, gathering like flies around a table, dribbling about things that don't matter."

"Maybe they matter to them," she said. "Maybe they would matter to me."

He laughed, shaking the car keys so the clanging overrode the ocean waves. "You're going to become one of them now? My little arty girl?" He gave her ear a little twist.

"I don't know what I want to become." She rose. "I thought I knew. Now I'm not so sure."

"You're just nervous about the wedding," he said. "When you walk down that aisle, you'll know everything."

She could see red bricks that made a path to the museum entrance as if it were a red carpet with poles strung in organdy leading up to a pulpit. She could hear the echoing voices and the soft sighs in the background. She could hear the words: *I promise to love, cherish, and to obey till death us do part.* It suddenly made her feel ill.

"That won't be for a while," she murmured.

He stared at her. "We're getting married in two weeks, remember?"

"No," she said carefully, "we're not."

His face turned white. "You're breaking our engagement?"

She looked at him, seeing in him a frightened little boy. "No, of course not. I'm postponing it."

"Because of your parents?" he asked.

"No," she said. "Because of me." She took his arm, feeling the breath return in her chest. "I'll explain it to you over lunch, dear."

He stared at her. "You're taking this whim of yours just a little too far, aren't you?"

"If it's too far, it's only to come back again," she said. "Out of the cage and a little more me."

As they made their way back to the car, the ocean across the street rolled out its waves like a white floor of wild daisies.

MOTHER OF MISCHIEF

"'There goes mother of mischief, running about, trying to get the world home.'" — Djuna Barnes, *Nightwood*

When Mary's brother Jim was eleven years old, he said to her one night, "You're Mother of Mischief."
Mary was sitting in the rocking chair swinging back and forth slowly like an old woman. She was startled out of her vague reverie watching the stars move across the night. She once wanted to learn about the constellations, but now it seemed like just watching them took more energy than she could muster.

"What do you mean?"

"You know."

It would be years before she would know.

Jim had good reason to say what he did. When her father was sent to fight in the Pacific , her mother alternated between tears and worry, locking herself in her room until dinnertime. The money her father had left them for their keep was stretched tight so there was nothing for a sitter, and they had no family or friends who could come and help. So Mary was left to watch over the rambunctious eight-year-old Jim and the needy three-year-old Rod.

Her brothers were good boys at heart. Jim helped her as much as he could with the salad or the potatoes when he came home from school. He was quick to spot her arched brow, her ankle thrust forward and her hands clasping her hips when he or Rod went too far and would remove them from her presence until she calmed down. But, being boys without responsibilities, they naturally fell into rascality.

They had food fights at the table and left her to clean up the mess. They shot spitballs at unsteady dishes sitting on the rack, making her rush to save them from shattering. Jim would come home from playing with his friends and run across the grain-colored carpet, his winter boots caked with mud. Once she tried to lock him out of the house until he cleaned them with the garden hose, but he snuck in through the cellar door.

One night in autumn, when Mary's father had been in the war for almost a year, her mother emerged from her room and sat with them at the dinner table. She hardly ate a morsel as she watched Mary dish out the food, hovering over Rod to cut his meat, scolding Jim for spilling his glass of milk. Her mother's tight little face showed mild recognition of the high-pitched voices around her, as if she realized for the first time in months these three people were her own offspring.

After the boys had gone to bed, Mary and her mother sat in the shabby living room, a choking fire going in the fireplace. Mary's hands grasped at the needle as she tried to darn one of Jim's socks. She was aware her mother was still watching her, her hands cupped inside her lap. Finally, her mother said in the creaky but soothing voice, "Your efforts won't be wasted, dear."

"I'm not so sure about that," Mary said with a laugh. "Jim goes through these socks as if he were pulling them through a meat grinder."

"I didn't mean the socks," said her mother. "I meant taking care of the boys." She looked wistfully into the dying fire. "Men need us in that way, you know."

"'Here is the House enclosing, the dear-loved dwelling place; Why should I ever weary for aught that I find not here?'" Mary quoted while carefully pulling the needle through the sock.

"Charlotte Perkins Gilman." Her mother smiled. "You remember."

"I can see now why you don't read me poetry anymore," Mary said. "Too much to do."

"I know it hasn't been easy, dear," said her mother. "I haven't been — well, I haven't been myself since your father's went overseas. We've never been out of one another's sight since I was eighteen. Thinking of him being halfway around the world and possibly in danger —" She gazed into the fire, her eyes soaking with tears.

Mary tossed the sock aside and took her mother's hand. "I know, Mom. I don't mind, really. They're good boys."

"I never had much, you know." Her mother smiled. "Your grandparents were good folks, but we were moving all the time." She chuckled. "Not much good making friends when you know you're going to shove off at any moment."

"But you got to see the country," Mary pointed out.

"I would much rather have made the little red house my world," she said. "That's where I was born — in a little red house. Bright red with faded pink walls and columns with angels carved on them."

Mary laughed, taking out a new thread. "Must have been owned once by a God-fearing madame."

Her mother did not smile. "Your father came along, and he was so sturdy, so exacting. He kept all his promises. All I ever wanted was to take care of him and you and your brothers." She sighed. "As it ought to be, I suppose."

"As it ought to be," Mary murmured.

"You'll see I'm right when you have that yourself, dear." Her mother squeezed her hand as she rose. "At least you'll be more prepared than most girls." As she trailed toward the stairs, her hand grasping the knob on the rail . "'To think of a thousand details, each in a thousand ways; For my own immediate people and a possible love and praise.'"

Mary looked up. "You said something, Mom?"

"I was just remembering Mrs. Gilman," she mused. The vague smile floated with the brightness of her eye as she made her way up the stairs.

The war ended not long after, and Mary's father returned home, shaken, but relieved and in good spirits. He went back to the newsstand and tobacco shop he had left in the capable hands of his partner, whose thick glasses had kept him out of battle.

Mary was happy that, once more, her mother's strength returned, her manner subdued, and her smile easy. For a few months, her mother went back to mothering and Mary could read her books again and concentrate on her studies instead of rushing through them to get to her home duties. She could even join her friends now and then at the local soda fountain to indulge in the latest school gossip and ogle the boys from the football team.

But all that came to a halt one night when, over dinner, Mary's father cleared his throat and, turning to her mother, said in that even tone of his that always signaled authority, "Edna, it's time we settled down."

"I don't know what you mean, dear," she said, amused. "We've been settled for some years, haven't we?"

"I'm talking about really settling," he said. "Pay up the mortgage, make those additions to the house we've always talked about. A man's got no business having kids if he's got nothing to leave them."

"Can I have my own room?" Jim piped up, edging his peas toward his mashed potatoes to hide them.

"'Course you can, son," he said, with a hearty laugh. "You and Mary. And one for little Roddy." He reached across the table and ruffled the little boy's golden head, making him laugh in a way that foretold of the heartiness he had inherited from his father.

"We haven't the money," his wife reminded him.

"That's where we all pitch in." George pointed a finger at her. "You had that job down at the diner before you married me, didn't you?"

Mary's mother nodded, putting more green peas onto Jim's plate, ignoring his frown. "Fred's always in need of extra help. Part-time, at least ."

"You'll have to go full-time," he said.

"Full-time!"

"We got no choice, honey." He covered her hand with his.

"But the children —"

"Mary's a fine little mother." He winked at his daughter. "You told me that yourself, didn't you?"

"But I'll be gone all day," his wife lamented.

"We can get someone to come in a few days a week to help with some of the housework," Mary's father said. "We can't afford more."

"Mary's never had to tend to the house and the boys for so long a time."

"Mary's got to learn it for the future anyway, doesn't she?" he said.

Her mother shrank in her chair. "The future's a long way off, George."

"Not so long," he insisted. "She's fourteen, isn't she?" He turned to his daughter. "You can do it, can't you, honey?"

"Sure, Daddy," she said. "Sure I can."

"I suppose we can ask Mrs. Miller to look in on them from time to time," Mary's mother lamented. "And Mrs. Freedman can come in twice a week to help with the house cleaning so Mary won't have too much to do."

"And Jim'll help, won't you Jim?" His father eyed him.

"'Course I will, Dad." There was almost a tone of eagerness in Jim's voice.

"Everyone's got to do their share." George helped himself to more of the ham. "Even little Roddy will do his when he gets old enough."

His wife stared. "You don't expect us to be in this situation for that long, do you?"

"All depends," he said vaguely.

"On what?" Mary asked. But her father only shrugged.

"Well, if you think it best, dear." Her mother sighed.

"It is best," he insisted. "It's for our children's future."

Later, Mary heard him mumbling into the folds of his paper, "Got to have a place. Got to leave 'em something, even if it ain't much."

In the years that followed, the idea of leaving something seemed to prey on her father's mind more than anything else. He left the house with the chill of the sunless sky and returned will the equal chill of night when all the porch lights on the block were burning. Her mother, too, worked long hours at the diner, often coming home with the scents of bacon and apple pie still clinging to her uniform.

It was then Mary became Mother of Mischief not only in body, but in mind and spirit. She chose not to finish her last year of high school. Her parents did not particularly like the idea but they didn't try to stop her. Even with Mrs. Freedman helping with the housework and the boys), the work Mary had to do made it difficult for her to concentrate on her books.

There were times when it frightened her how much she didn't miss school when she caught snatches of flying chatter from her former classmates as they passed her by at the store or on the street. Their talk of ankle-strap shoes and the latest hit from Jimmy Dorsey's band were like a foreign language to her.

She didn't give up her reading entirely but much of it became fashion magazines and romance novels. Sometimes, when the dim of evening fell and her brothers were in bed, she wandered to the the bookshelf and ran her hand along the spines, thinking of how she had strained her eyes over Gilman and Dickinson and Millay with a flashlight under the covers well past her bedtime when she was a child. How superfluous they all seemed to her now in the grind of everyday life!

She turned eighteen and the few young men who had eyed her in school went off to college. Now older men in town looked at her, seeing her as the perfect match with their ideas of a future wife. She felt them watching her as she directed and scolded her brothers in the stores or at the park. They were mostly shy, retired men who approached her with tentative gazes, hinting more than asking her out for dinner or to the latest picture show. She always declined hurriedly, her mind on the vacuuming she still had to do or contemplating if she put less baking soda in the biscuits, her father wouldn't complain about them being so heavy. Always, there was some thought pushing aside these men's coveted offers. When she got home and mulled over them, a feeling of dread seeped through her at the idea of marriage.

Her father's eyesight began to fail, and her mother's crooked posture made her look like a hunchback as she walked into the house after her shift. Dinner was now a silent affair, sometimes punctuated with the clanging and pounding of workers putting up new rooms in the house. Her parents were too exhausted to worry about what was happening with the boys and relied on Mary to do the fretting and fussing. This she did, with the expertise of one who had raised ten children. She did the scolding when Rod became too fidgety or took his brother's things without permission. And, the night Jim announced his intentions to enlist to fight the war in Korea, she was the one whose coffee cup came smashing down on the kitchen floor in horror while her mother simply looked glossy-eyed into the steam coming from the hot water while she helped Mary do the dishes.

"You're only sixteen!"

"I don't mean *now*," Jim shrugged. "When I'm eighteen, of course."

Her beating heart began to ease. "Oh, by that time, it'll all be over."

"I might enlist anyway," he sulked.

"You said you wanted to run a big company like US Steel and make lots of money." She held the clean plate in both her hands. "You've been saying that since you were six."

"Well, I changed my mind!" He threw down the apple in his hand. "Bud said you can see the world in the army."

"Did he also tell you that you can get killed while you see the world?"

"Women don't understand!"

For the first time that evening, their mother spoke. "Your father didn't like the army."

"That's 'cause he had to go, Mom," he said. "I'd go because I want to."

"You're talking nonsense, Jim," Mary said. "You won't go, not now and not when you're eighteen."

He stood silently looking at her while she carefully scrubbed the oily platter and dried every corner. "You do that like it's your life's work," he mumbled and slithered out of the kitchen.

Something in his voice made her hold the platter like a baby, feeling the glass warm from the steaming water against her hands.

She waited each day for the love and praise her mother had once promised her to come from Jim and Rod. But none did. On the night that led her to think about marrying Walter, one of the more persistent of the older men, she realized none would.

By that time, her brothers had not only become experts at evading the Mother of Mischief pose but resisting any sort of mothering. They scarcely needed taking care of, but Mary couldn't seem to let go. She chased after them, cleaned their rooms, dug the dirty laundry from under their beds, and gave their friends the sort of lunches their own mothers considered too fussy. She expected her brothers to recognize that, with their father busy day and night and their mother now head waitress at the diner, there was one person who tried to curtail the dangers teenage boys could run into because of too much mischief. And there were times when they were grateful, kissing her cheek lovingly and murmuring, "Thanks, Sis," for everything she did.

But more often, they weren't. Rod hardly gave her more than a blank stare in the mornings, ignoring the breakfast she set out for him in favor of a sliver of toast loaded with butter perched in one hand while he grabbed his books in the other and headed off to school. Jim would walk into the kitchen and glance down at the steaming plate of scrambled eggs and bacon and the waffles marking the air with their sweet scent. He would push them away, give her a look of resentment, and walk out of the house to the high school a few blocks away. Their silence sent a shiver through her spine more than their rejection of the hot breakfast. It was the same silence she endured pacing the carpet when they were boys, watching at the window for their pale blue bicycles to emerge from over the hill just as the streetlights were flickering on. It was the sort of silence one gave an intruder.

The night she decided to marry Walter, she found herself waiting for them to come home. Lately, she had begun to fear that one day, they would never come home. She sat on the porch in the same rocking chair she frequented during the war, its legs creaking like an old dog's, and, rocking to and fro, she waited. She waited while the late afternoon sun bore into the surface of her skin and marked it with a polished red. She waited when the cap of cobalt sky turned to beetle black, and the stars appeared as jewels just as they always had.

Rod came first before dinner turned cold. He was more amiable than he had been in the morning, but tired, dragging his school books over his shoulder.

"I told you to be home by three!" Lately, her voice had taken on a razor edge and came out ringing too gruff for a woman of twenty-one.

"Told you, bowling with Bobby and Mike," he mumbled.

"Until dark?"

"It's not that dark yet," he sulked.

"Mom worries about you."

His head shot up. "Mom isn't here."

"All right, then, *I* worry about you." She tried to lighten her tone. "A thirteen-year-old shouldn't be out this late at night."

"It's not night. It's late evening." He had acquired the habit of exact words, something she imagined he picked up from his friends.

"Six o'clock is night!" she insisted. "And dinner is at five-thirty. I want you home by three from now on."

"You've no right to tell me what to do. No right at all," he mumbled, slinking into the house before she could answer.

She sat back, feeling her fingers grow stiff as they dug into the arms of the chair. Adolescence seemed to have taken a greater toll on him than his brother. Not so long ago, he would have come home on time, waving to her, smiling, and telling her about his day, then asking about hers and listening attentively to the answer.

But as she sat there creaking away, to and fro, to and fro, she imagined those past conversations, seeing them like a film unrolling in her mind, one frame at a time. She realized that a year or so ago, he started to pull away from her. There had been a too-formal politeness in his voice when he spoke to her, and as she relayed to him the events of her day, he didn't even bother to look at her. His eyes wandered instead into the garden they'd planted during the war. The tomatoes were sagging now and the squash was pitted as if bugs had gotten at them.

She waited for Jim to come home. He finally showed up when the moon was well risen in the sky. The wheat hair that had been so fine when he was a boy stood like straw all around his head and his lanky figure was beginning to adjust to the broad-shoul-dered frame of a seventeen-year-old. He walked with a swagger of arrogance befitting his age but in a manner that implied he would soon grow out of it.

Mary stopped rocking and sat very straight in the chair. "Where in God's name have you been?"

"Don't take the Lord's name in vain," he said warily.

"Don't give me any lip, Jim," she snapped. "You're late."

"For what?" He ran his hand through his hair.

She looked at him, startled. "Why, for dinner, of course."

"Am I a baby that needs to be fed on time?"

"Really, Jim."

"You're always trying to stuff us." He slung his book bag over his left shoulder. "And not only with food. All those blankets you put on our beds choke us at night."

"Don't speak for your brother." Her voice sounded like a thread against the heavy black night.

"Someone ought to speak up," he said. "We're not your sons, Mary. And we're not your husband either."

She could barely see him as he had moved away from the porch light, enveloped in shadows. But Jim inherited their father's sharp blue eyes, the only one who had, and she could feel them cutting into her like knives through the dark.

She lowered her voice. "Jim, you're not as grown up as you think you are."

"I'm not a child!" he boomed. "Lots of boys my age pass for eighteen and go off to Korea."

Her blood froze. "I thought that was settled."

"It was settled with you, not with me."

"Is that what you really want to do?"

"If I do," he said, pulling at some dry leaves from a plant on the porch. "It will be your fault."

"My fault!"

"You suffocate us," he growled. "Rod says he feels like you have a muzzle over us, leading us around by the leash like naughty dogs."

"Men and boys need taking care of," she found herself saying, hearing the echo of her mother's voice.

He had moved under the light and now leaned against the screen door, studying her. "What do you get out of it?"

"What?"

"I said, what do you get out of it?"

She blinked into the darkness. "Why, it's my duty. I'm the older sister."

"Mary, isn't it time you stopped being Mother of Mischief?" he asked. "You ought to marry Walter, you know."

"Walter!"

"He'd ask you quick enough," he said. "Always buzzing around whenever we're at Creel & Sons."

"Why should I marry Walter?"

"He's a nice fellow," said her brother. "Got a big house and a shiny car and everything."

"He's almost forty if he's a day," she sniffed.

"Men and boys need taking care of," he mocked.

"How dare you make fun of me!" she screeched. "After everything I do for you and Rod."

"It's hardly a prize when we didn't ask for it." He carefully opened the front door, letting the screen shut behind himself.

"That's not the point."

"It's exactly the point," he insisted. "Marry Walter. I'll bet he'll ask for it." His eyes arched. "Or is it that you're afraid?"

"I'm not afraid of marrying Walter or anyone else," she snarled.

"I meant afraid of yourself," he said. "Afraid of who you might be if you stopped being Mother of Mischief."

She wanted to answer him, to chide him about how unappreciative he and Rod were of how she had given up so much of her life, her schooling, and her reading, for them. She wanted the pedestal her mother had promised her with their shining faces glowing with accolades and gratitude. She wanted the love and praise for the thousand little details she thought of in a thousand ways for the thousands of days she had thought of them. If not from them, then perhaps from someone.

So she married Walter. He was thirty-nine at their wedding, a man on the thick-waisted side, though pleasantly so, but his face was still smooth and his smile unfailing. No one seemed the wiser of their eighteen-year difference. Her parents had sighed with relief when she told them.

"It will be security for you, dear." Her mother embraced her. "Your red house with pink painted walls, remember?"

"And the angels carved in the columns," Mary said, smiling.

"Makes a good living," her father remarked, chewing at the end of his pipe. "Sober man. Can't ask for more than that."

Only Rod seemed to protest. "He's probably one of those 'still waters run deep' fellows," he said. "If you have kids, he'll be rickety and old by the time they go to college."

"He's not so bad," Jim insisted. "They say he took good care of his mother until she died." He eyed Mary but said no more than that, as if they shared some secret between them since the night he had urged her to marry Walter.

She moved into the house Walter's mother had left him, one of the most elegant in Rawlins. The Queen Anne style was a little ornate for Mary's taste and Walter, in his generous way, offered to sell it and move into something more modern. Touched by his eagerness to please her, she laid her hand in his. "I wouldn't think of it. If your mother loved it, so will I."

"They used to envy Ma in the village." He always referred to Rawlins as a "village." "Sterling used to stick his head out of the window every time he saw her walking down the street and make her an offer. Those real estate hounds know a good thing when they see it."

Mary soon realized she was the envy of some of the ladies in town. Walter adored cars and bought her a peach-colored Chrysler and as she slid into town to do her shopping, a few removed their sunglasses to admire it. The Queen Anne's scrolls and arabesques hid modern trimmings inside the house, and Walter insisted they renovate the kitchen. The fancy countertops and appliances could have leapt off the page of *Better Homes and Gardens*. When Mary's mother first saw it, tears filled her eyes. A lump formed in Mary's throat as she thought of how close her mother was now to the red house of her dreams.

For the first four years of their marriage, their lives took on a pleasant routine. In the early morning, Walter would set out to Creel & Sons where he was head of the shoe department. Mary's life shifted from the narrow walls of her parents' home to the bright white of the Queen Anne. She finished her housework by the afternoon, but when she tried to pick up one of the books she once loved, the words blurred and her head began to ache. So she spent the time until Walter came home wandering around the house, finding corners her dust rag had missed, picking coils of yarn from her evening knitting off the carpet. Usually, she found something they needed and rushed off to the grocery store or hardware store or some small shop in town, arriving home in plenty of time to make dinner for Walter.

She would pass Creel & Sons every day, deliberately going up the side alley where the shoe department could be seen from the windows. She would often find Walter attending to customers, bending over them with his eager eyes and winning smile. But she never waved, reluctant to interrupt a sale. She never told him of her daily excursions to the store.

In the evening, he came home at six without fail, but the years with her brothers and their unpredictable habits conditioned her to peer out the open window, her hands folded on the sill, searching the street for the Fedora he always wore.

She wasn't sure when she first felt the change in him. She only knew she began to notice the eager smile had a touch of irony in it, and when she took his hat and coat, pushed his slippers and dressing gown into his hands, and told him to wash up because dinner would be in ten minutes, he looked almost offended. She brushed aside her uneasiness, and yet, she could not help but feel her attention sharpen from the moment he came home until they went to bed. Her alert eyes grew stiffer and more disturbed when she passed the store window, though there was nothing amiss about Walter's manner toward his customers, nothing she could put her finger on.

One night, as they retired to the living room after dinner, he looked up from his paper and demanded, "What do you think I'm doing in that store all day?"

"Working, of course, dear," she said with a small smile.

"I saw you looking through the window. See you every day, in fact." Then he leaned forward and said in his gentle way, "You shouldn't do that, honey. Mr. Hardy saw you today too. He thinks you're distracting me."

"But I never even wave," she protested.

"It isn't that, dear," he said. "It's like when a blind man looks at you in the street, and you know he's seeing you as some-thing, but you don't know what. It's — it's antagonizing!" He spit the word out. "And don't look out the window like that, either."

"Like what?"

"Like you're waiting with bated breath for me to open the front door."

"I have to see when you get home to make sure I don't put the dressing on the salad too early."

"Well, don't I always come home at six?" He took up his pipe and gnawed on the end. "You'd think I was one of the boys carousing in the bar after work so that I can face the wife and kiddies. Some of those guys' wives are just the limit."

"I can't help it, Walter." She put down the cap she was knitting and stared through the flames in the fireplace. "I'm Mother of Mischief, you see."

"Who?"

She grimaced. "Jim used to call me that."

"Well, what does it mean?"

She blinked, realizing she had no answer. She only said, "It's who I am."

Mary did try to keep from passing the store window. For this, she had to avoid going out for most of the day. She grew restless, her hands fidgeting through the housework and her eyes gliding around as if she were searching for the last vestige of comfort, like a child looking for her favorite toy. When she did go out, her steps grew heavy as she passed the corner where the department store stood. It took all her strength not to run to the window when the clock in the living room chimed six.

In the end, she found herself passing by the store window when Walter's attention was averted, and keeping the window curtains closed but leaving just enough of a crack so she could see the street but those in the street could not see her.

One evening, the clock struck six just as she was placing a cherry pie, Walter's favorite, on a cooling rack. She approached the window, wiping her hands on a towel slung over her shoulder. Her husband was across the street chatting with their neighbor, Dottie Fry, and her daughter Judy. They were all laughing. Dottie had her arms crossed, and Judy leaned against the swinging door of the heavy iron gate.

Suddenly, Judy climbed onto the gate, and started chattering to Walter. Though Mary couldn't hear the words, she watched as he swung her back and forth. The girl threw her head around with glee, her blond ponytail swinging like a tongue of a grandfather clock and her bangs blowing in the wind. All three looked as delighted as school children on a playground.

She went downstairs, thinking she would go out to meet him. But as her hand grasped the door knob, she stopped. There had been something forbidding about them gathered around the gate like that. A lightness of being, something like the three little cats she had once seen inside a snow globe in a catalogue. The cats were gathered with their hats and scarves and mittens, holding their paws in prayer and their large eyes shut in contentment. A little covenant of delight and comfort that had the ring of Christmas in it. Just now, watching the trio playing with the gate, laughing, and seeing Walter with his cheeks ruddy and his eyes in a way she had not seen for a while, she was reminded of those three cats.

She returned to the kitchen and lingered over the pork chops, stirring the apple sauce that went with them. It seemed almost hours before she heard the rattling of the front door and Walter whistling as he came in, though she knew it had only been minutes.

His cheerfulness gave her a feeling of anticipation, and she grabbed the slippers and dressing gown already laid out on the chair. But when she approached him, a look of annoyance crossed his face.

"You're always fluttering around when I get home," he snapped. "Can't you stand still while I get settled?" He started to slip the coat off his shoulders, and she caught the collar and eased it down his arms. "Mary, please!"

"I'm sorry," she said. "It's just nice to have some noise in the house."

He gave her an amused glance as he hung up the coat. "I'm glad I'm good for something."

"I didn't mean that, dear," she said. "I mean, it's just nice to have you home. You bring a warmth into the house. It's cold, being here alone all day." She shivered.

"Yes, it's nice to have people to talk to," he mused as he untied his shoes and laid them in the corner near the coat rack.

"Is that why you're home so late?"

His entire bulk grew rigid. "It's only a twenty past six."

"Last week, you were home by six," she reminded him. "When we were first married, you used to try and make it home by five-thirty."

"I had fewer responsibilities at the store then," he said. "Now, well, they expect me to stay and see to the clearing up. Can't leave shoes and things lying around, can you? What would the customers think?" He patted her cheek.

"And that's all?" she said. "Just the shoes?"

"Isn't it enough?" He glanced at her. "You never understood much about the retail business, Mary. A store's got to be as clean and organized as, well — this house." He threw a glance around. "Don't crowd me, dear. I've had a hard day. Had to chew out one of the junior salesmen for short-changing a customer. I practically flew home just so I wouldn't be later than I am."

Her stomach grew tight as she thought of the scene she had just witnessed outside the window. But she only said, "Dinner in ten minutes."

"I'll be ready." He headed up the stairs.

They ate the soup in silence. She watched as he made small slurping sounds, wondering when he had acquired that habit. It seemed lately he had acquired many habits she had never noticed before, like wearing flannel socks, though he said their thickness always put the shoe out of sorts, and watching television well after she had gone to bed.

"Have you always eaten your soup that way?" she asked suddenly.

His head jerked up. "What way?"

"Oh, it doesn't matter."

"You have the oddest ideas sometimes, Mary." He moved the rolls closer to him.

"I was always told I had a good mind," she mused. "Walter, do you suppose you'll get your promotion soon?"

He stared at her. "What promotion?"

"The one you've been working so hard for," she said. "At least, I assume you're working hard for it, coming home late like that."

"It was only twenty minutes!" he growled. "I linger sometimes, it's true. But I told you once, most of the boys go out for a beer before heading home. I never do. I come straight home to you."

Feeling herself weighed down under the exasperating silence, she tried to make her voice light as she remarked, "Well, you didn't come straight home tonight. You stopped to chat with the Frys."

The serving spoon tilted in his hand, and a few green beans fell onto the tablecloth. She picked them up with a napkin, then went for a wet cloth to rub out the butter stain. Only when she sat down again did he answer, "How did you know I was talking to Mrs. Fry?"

"I was putting the pie to cool, and I saw you through the window." Her tongue felt dry, though she knew it wasn't exactly a lie.

He gave her a sharp look. "You can't see the Fry house from the kitchen window."

"All right, I was looking out the upstairs window," she admitted. "But it was getting late, and I was worried."

His shoulders dropped a little as he took a potato from the warm dish. "We weren't talking about anything special, dear. I heard a funny joke today, and I was just telling her about it."

"I hope it wasn't a dirty joke," she said. "In front of the child."

"Oh, you saw Judy too?" He spread the roll with butter.

"Yes, I saw Judy too."

"She isn't a child, by the way," he said. "She'll be graduating next year and going to college."

"Then why were you swinging her on the gate?"

His eyes slid past her. "It was just a bit of fun."

"Do you think we ought to be encouraging a friendship with them, Walter?" She took a sip of coffee. "Considering what they are."

"What they are?" he echoed. "They're our neighbors. Mrs. Fry always used to bring 'round a coffee cake at Christmas time for Ma when she was alive."

"I didn't mean to imply she wasn't nice." Mary lowered her voice. "But you can't deny she hasn't the cleanest reputation in town."

"Maybe not among your friends," he snapped.

"I don't have friends," she said honestly. "But I do stop to chat with the ladies now and then. And they say she was, well, rather wild in her youth."

"Nonsense." He sawed through the pork chop. "Mrs. Fry isn't what you think she is. She's very active in the church."

"How do you know?" she challenged.

"She was telling me about the church bazaar on Sunday." He put down his fork.

"Be that as it may," said Mary, "I don't approve of her. I've nothing against the woman, really. But I'm sure you wouldn't want your wife associating with a divorcée."

"She's a widow," he insisted. "Her husband died in the war."

"Oh, she *says* he did." Mary leaned forward with her elbows on the table. "But some people in town don't think so."

"You ought to go back to reading books, dear," he said with a note of wariness. "They'll feed your imagination much better than those magpies."

The glance he gave her made her feel humbled, and she realized she had been lashing out at a woman who had never been anything but cordial to her. "I'm sorry," she said. "I'm sure she's a nice person. I didn't mean to sound disagreeable."

"You're never that, Mary." There was a slight catch in his voice.

"I do think she ought to get married again." She poured him more coffee, though his cup was half-full. "Maybe we could get Mr. Stiller to come here for dinner one night and invite her and her daughter. That ought to open some doors."

His fork dropped in his plate. "Really, Mary. I do think the woman is capable of handling her own affairs."

"That might be the trouble," she said. "The ladies say she was quite a 'woman of affairs' in her youth. One of those flappers, I take it, weighed down by beads and bootleggers."

He snapped his head back and laughed. For the first time in a long time, she saw he was truly amused, as his apple face glistened with hilarity. "I was wrong. You shouldn't be reading books. You should be a fiction writer for *Woman's Day* or one of those magazines you're always leafing through at the drugstore."

She felt a sting in her eyes as she began collecting the dishes. "I haven't time, Walter. The house has me tied up from morning until night."

"I've told you a million times, I'm more than willing to hire a maid." His voice was raised so she could hear it echo in the kitchen as she soaked the dishes and began to cut the pie. "You told me once you used to help your mother organize the church socials every year."

"That was before she had to work to help give us something," said Mary.

"Before you became Mother of Mischief," he murmured.

"I suppose you're going to tell me Judy gives up her Sundays to go pray in the church with her mother?" she snarled.

There was a pause of silence. "I don't know them well enough to answer that question."

"I don't like that girl," she called back. "I think her mother lets her bleach her hair."

"Mary, for heaven's sake!"

She emerged from the kitchen, the pie in her hands. "And I've seen her coming home late at night with a boy on her arm." She cocked her head. "And not always the same boy either."

His comfortable figure stiffened, as if he had grown a few inches taller. "You've been spying on them!"

"Heavens, no," she insisted. "But I do lock the windows at

night, and I can see their house very clearly. She ought not to allow Judy to stay out so late." Her voice trailed away.

"All the kids do that nowadays." Walter said. "It's the age of independence for those young'uns."

"Well, I think it's wrong." She settled in her chair. "Especially for a girl. It was bad enough for Joe, but a girl starts to develop a reputation when she's that age. And if it isn't the right one —"

"She gets tarred and feathered?" he asked warily.

She crushed the fork into the pie. "If you were a woman, you would understand."

"I haven't heard any complaints about how Mrs. Fry has been raising her daughter," he said firmly. "I feel for the woman. It couldn't have been easy for her, all alone."

"Perhaps that's why she's so cheap," Mary growled.

The fork dropped in his plate again. "How can a woman who is active in her church be cheap?"

"You sound as if you'd like *me* to be active in the church," she snarled.

"Why not?" He looked at her. "You ought to get out more, Mary. You told me you enjoyed those socials."

"A woman starts going out, she becomes cheap, like Mrs. Fry and her girl."

He threw the napkin on the table. "That's not fair, Mary. It's not even decent."

"Is it decent for her to go around in those frilly dresses and magenta lipstick and cat's-eyed glasses and let her daughter drive a convertible?" Mary snapped. "Is it decent for the girl to come home with boys on weekend nights? You can be so blind, Walter!"

"I would have hoped you, of all people, would have some sympathy for her," he said.

"Why me especially?"

"Because you practically raised your brothers," he said. "I should think you would know what it's like to have to care for a child."

The remark left a bitter note in the air like some foul plant. She picked up the coffee cup, feeling it tremble in her hand. "Those days are gone, Walter. That's what I got married for."

"What about our own child?" The words dropped like marbles on the maplewood table. "That's what you really need, Mary. With all your — well, nurturing qualities."

"Funny," she mused. "Jim told me those same nurturing qualities would be better served as a wife."

"And now I'm telling you they would be well served as a mother." His voice was harsh.

"Well, we haven't been trying very hard lately, have we?" She glared at him.

He rose. "No. We haven't."

She studied his face. It wasn't an entirely unappealing face, though the ruddiness was gone now, replaced by a few wrinkles and freckles that hadn't been there before. She suddenly realized Walter would be fifty in a few years. "We could try again," she ventured. "I would love a child or two. However many you want. Whatever you want, Walter."

He blinked at her. A mark of indifference made his face look like a mask. "Right now, all I want is to read the paper and get close to the fire. It's chilly tonight, isn't it?" His voice was softer than it had been earlier, but the wrinkles on his face remained.

He left her to clear the table and do the dishes as he always did, and wandered into the living room. She heard him whistling again as he opened the paper and crushed tobacco into his pipe. The glow in the house was warm with the lemon-colored bulbs against the black sky peering from behind the window curtains. This time of day always gave her a retiring feeling, as if all were in balance again — her husband was home, well fed, relaxing with his paper and pipe. But tonight, she felt agitation sticking pins in her from their conversation and its stinging words. She feared they would make welts in her skin that would not heal.

She bent over the dishes in the sink, her eyes narrow. It was her favorite chore. She liked to feel the warm water lapping over her hands, the bounciness of the soap bubbles, and the satisfaction of watching the grease and sauce and butter cleared from the china as she set the dishes on the rack. But tonight, washing dishes held no comfort for her.

Walter hadn't mentioned the idea of a baby for some time. In their first year of marriage, the idea of having a baby had taken up their married life. They had occupied their free hours with counting days and making anxious visits to the doctor. She had watched every young mother her age in the stores, carefully maneuvering baby carriages, cooing to the tiny inhabitant nestled inside, inspecting toys and clothes as if they wished they could afford to buy them. But lately, she and Walter had resigned themselves to childlessness, and neither was interested in reviving the hope of having a baby. She had stopped noticing the young mothers and their carriages long ago.

The serving dish slipped from her hands and fell into the sink with a clatter. She felt the same frozen blood in her veins as the night Jim confronted her about letting go of Mother of Mischief. Her hands didn't warm to the water nor bend easily around the dishes as she turned them over to scrub with soap. They were numb, as was her heart. As she picked up the platter, she realized how dejected she felt. Dropped from Jim's hands, from Rod's. But a woman's husband didn't drop her, she reminded herself as she soaped the platter. Marriage was forever.

She finished the dishes and went into the living room. Walter's face was buried behind the paper. She sat on the couch, staring at her knitting basket. She took it up, smoothing down the folds of the sweater she was knitting. In a low voice so as not to jar him out of his reading, she said, "You're right, honey. We ought to have had a baby a long time ago."

"It doesn't matter now, dear." He spoke from behind the paper.

"It's my fault," she lamented. "I never told you — I ought to have told you — but I didn't feel ready for a child."

He let the paper drop and stared at her. "Mother of Mischief not ready for a baby?"

"Maybe it's *because* I was Mother of Mischief that I wasn't ready." She set the knitting aside. "I want to try and explain."

"So, explain." A note of impatience entered his voice.

"I was Mother of Mischief since I was twelve," she began. "My mother had — well I guess you would call it a nervous break-down — when my father went off to the Pacific, and I had to take over caring for Jim and Rod, at least partly."

"I know all that, sweetheart," he said.

"And then when Dad came home, I thought it would be over, but it wasn't." She felt as if the gray night floating into the room. "Mom had to go to work, and I was expected to help take care of the boys. I never had much of a childhood, you see."

"What has that to do with having a baby?" Walter stifled a yawn.

Her nerves felt grated now. "When we got married, I just wanted to be alone with you. Get used to being a wife, you know. I still feel that way."

"I understand." His voice sounded oddly polite. "If you're not ready for a child, honey, that's all right. You're young and we can wait." He picked up the newspaper again.

"A woman needs time to be different," she murmured. But he had already become engrossed in the sports page.

~~~~~

The next day, she went to the church her parents still frequented and asked the preacher if he had anything she could do. He sent her to his wife, who was only too glad to have another volunteer. She put Mary to work with the children who had been placed by working mothers into the church daycare. She found herself running around, her hands grasping every-thing all at once as they had when her brothers were little boys. The little girls seemed content to play with their dolls or draw, but the boys howled and ran away from her.
~~~~~

One little boy grabbed some finger paints and began to spill them all over the floor, then got down on his hands and knees and smeared the colors all together, laughing like a clown. Mary stood over him, assuming her Mother of Mischief pose. The little boy looked up, tall in her baby doll pumps and pencil skirt, with her hand on her hip and one foot jutted out as if ready to tap on the floor with stern reprimand. He stopped painting and allowed himself to be led to the church bathroom to wash his hands.

The rest of the afternoon the boy watched Mary with pebble eyes. They reminded her of the eyes of a grizzly bear in a series of children's books she used to read to Rod when he was a child. The eyes had always pressed themselves into the dark when she went to bed, glowing green eyes watching her in her sleep and making her toss and turn. She thought at first the little boy was angry with her, and she tried to approach him with a kind word, then with an apple and a coloring book. But he hunched his shoulders and pressed himself into a ball, the repudiation so complete it made her cringe.

She came home in the afternoon, her head and feet aching from all the running around. She made a detour near the store, trying to get a glimpse of Walter's round face, and saw he was helping a customer. An array of penny loafers, saddle shoes, and moccasins lay scattered around him as he bent down, opening a box to extract a pair of low-heeled strap shoes. The smile on his face was broader than she had seen in a long time, and his features jumped as he spoke to the customer in an animated tone. She could almost feel the vibrations of his booming voice against the store window. She came a few steps closer and saw the customer was Judy Fry.

That night after they had settled in the living room after dinner, Walter examined his pipe a moment and said, "I'm beginning to think you're right, dear."

"About what?" She looked up, feeling the weight of the yarn from the sweater she was making.

"Judy Fry does seem a little — well, maybe she's been too wild lately," he admitted. "Mrs. Fry was telling me the other day how much Judy misses her father."

"I'm sure she does." Mary went back to her knitting.

"I think I should offer to give her a hand," he said. "Just a little paternal advice when I see her from time to time, you know."

"I don't see any reason why you shouldn't."

He glanced at her. "You've certainly changed your tune since the other night."

"I was being unkind," she said. "I see that now. It takes all kinds in this world, as Mom used to say."

"Then you don't mind?"

"I think it's a nice thing for you to do, Walter," she said. "Perhaps the girl needs some fatherly guidance."

After that, she started passing by the store window again. She saw Judy there often, buying socks or looking at the hosiery with one school friend or another. Sometimes she was by herself. Always, Walter looked the same as he had that first time she'd seen the girl there.

The winter months flew by and spring arrived. Mary eventually stopped her work at the daycare and began attending her garden with a passion. She cleared the front yard of weeds and dry vegetation and spent time at the nursery consulting with Mr. and Mrs. Clark on the best flowers and vegetables for their soil. The geraniums bloomed for a few days before they began to drift downward as if the blood color were draining from their petals. The roses attracted so many bugs she had to pull them out of the ground. But the tomatoes ripened and grew plump and heart-shaped, sending their fresh scent throughout the garden.

Mary felt her chest swell with pride as she gathered them in a basket, their skins filmed with dust. She had been itching to make a tomato salad from a recipe she had found in a magazine since the green buds appearing on the vines. She spent the afternoon carefully chopping the tomatoes so the pieces would be perfectly sized the way Walter liked his salads.

But he hardly noticed. He did little more than grunt when she gloated over her accomplishment with the tomatoes. He had, in fact, been very distracted lately. He went out in the morning and came back in the evening at the same times as always, spoke to her in the same manner, sat with his paper and pipe after dinner in the same way. He had even become a little more attentive toward her, fixing things around the house that she had been needling him about for months and taking her to the movies once in a while. The previous week they had even laughed over a story she told him about Rod when he was a little boy.

But that night, he was as remote from her as if he were sitting on the other side of the world instead of right across the dinner table. He chewed slowly, giving her mechanical complements on the food though she knew he wasn't really tasting anything. He kept staring past her, his eyes glassy and contemplative.

She ventured, "Something wrong at the store, dear?"

"Nothing," he murmured.

"You seem preoccupied tonight." She played with the casserole on her plate. "You've been working too hard these past months. We ought to go away somewhere this summer. Maybe Catalina."

"Summer?" he echoed.

"Everyone will be away in August anyway," she said. "Kids out of school and all. Mrs. Fallow was telling me that she and Roger are going to take the kids to Disneyland."

"Yes." He cleared his throat. "Yes. Well, Mary, the fact is, I'll be going away this summer too. Even sooner."

"*You'll* be going away?" She gave a little laugh. "Don't you mean *we'll* be going away?"

"No," he said. "I don't."

She reached for the tomato salad. "I don't understand."

"No, I'm sure you don't." His voice rose a little. "I've never been what you call eloquent."

"Maybe we can try to get away every weekend when summer comes," she said, excited Walter was showing interest in the idea of a vacation. "Just little trips, you know. There's so much to see around here, and you're always saying I don't get out of the house enough —"

"Mary!" The screech in his voice alarmed her, and she looked at him, startled. "Mary," he continued, steadying his voice. "I want a divorce."

The fork and knife slipped from her hands. "I don't understand."

"That's just the trouble," he said. "You don't understand anything. You only know how to do, not understand. Oh!" He yanked the napkin from his lap and it fell to the floor. "I'm not blaming you. I'm not blaming anybody." He rubbed his hands together. "I'm in love with Judy."

It was as if a million bees had entered the house and were buzzing around her, incessant and hounding. Her head reeled. "She's a child!"

"She'll be eighteen soon," he said. "She finishes school next month. And, well, when she's eighteen, we'd like to get married."

She began laughing. "You're married to me!"

"That's what I'm trying to tell you." His voice was gentle. "I want to be unmarried to you."

"Don't condescend to me!" she screamed.

"I'm trying to explain." He licked his lips. "We never meant for it to happen. I wanted to be a father to her, really. But something changed between us —"

"I don't want to hear it." She closed her eyes.

"You're right." He sighed. "It hardly matters now. I'm packing my things tonight and going to a hotel. I'll get out of town so there won't be any talk."

"To think you've been having an affair with a child all this time —" She held her head in her hands.

"We did not have an affair!" The voice became steel. "It was never anything like that. I never touched her, and she never wanted me to. I told you, it just happened!"

"I've done everything I was supposed to, didn't I?" The words sounded thick against her tongue, as if it were half paralyzed.

"It isn't a question of what you've done or haven't done." He pressed his hands together. "We were never in love, Mary. Let's face the facts."

"The facts," she said. "This clean house is a fact. Your clean clothes are a fact. This dinner is a fact. That fire in the fireplace is a fact."

"You're not making sense."

"No, I guess I'm not," she murmured. "She only said 'possible love and praise.' She never made any promises, did she?"

"Who?"

"Charlotte Anna Perkins Gilman." Mary's eyes widened, and she felt as if they would never shut again.

He gazed at her for a minute. Then, he continued, "I don't want you worrying about money. You can keep the house. I promised to take care of you and I will."

"Yes," she said. "Security. Security, love, and praise. All a woman has, Mom said."

"This is the best thing, Mary." He laid a hand on hers. "You'll see."

"Where have my thousand details gone?" she lamented. Then, suddenly a bomb exploded inside her, racking her bones. "You never appreciated everything I did! You were all supposed to appreciate it!" The screams tore from her throat.

In a quiet voice, he said, "People rarely appreciate what they don't ask for."

She stared at him, her breath caught. "That's what Jim said."

"He's a smart young man," said Walter. He bent down and

picked the napkin off the floor, folding it neatly into a square. "He always has been."

"Am I supposed to live with that?" She glared at him.

"We each have to live with ourselves, Mary." He rose. "The saint and the satan in us."

After he left, the buzzing in her head ceased and all was quiet. The house felt suddenly eerie. Whatever ghosts had been lurking behind the walls suddenly come out. They were all staring at her, their eyes glowing like the bear that had frightened her as a child.

She stumbled to her feet and began collecting the dishes. Clattering around the dinnerware and cleaning the smears of casserole and butter gave her a feeling of familiarity. The remaining ripe tomatoes sat in a bowl in the center of the kitchen table where she placed it so she could see it every time she entered, a reminder of her accomplishment. They leered at her now like big red eyes.

She suddenly grabbed one and threw it at the wall. It smashed into a explosion of juice, pulp, and seeds. She covered her face with her hands still dirty from the tomato, the dust mixing with her tears.

It seemed like hours before her tears ran dry. She could hear Walter's heavy footsteps upstairs as he packed his things. He had always been a slow-moving man, deliberating every step as if it was bringing him closer to the gallows. But, tonight, his walk was more assured.

Mary wiped her face with a towel and went into the living room where her purse lay on the table. She took out a compact and lipstick and redid her make up, feeling a little calmer. Then, she took out the keys to the Chrysler.

She drove at a steady speed though her heart was racing. Grasping the steering wheel, she saw the blank face of Judy Fry through the windshield. How innocent it was, how untouched! It wasn't that she had no signs of age. It was that she had no signs of pain and burden. Nothing had worn down her resistance, enthusiasm, and zest for life. Mary couldn't help but wonder what she would be like in twenty years.

She crossed the Bay Bridge to Harrison Street and found herself climbing the hills of San Francisco higher and higher until she reached the summit of Twin Peaks. The layers of the city were hidden with the night but lights melted into a tapestry of diamonds spilling onto a velvet blanket. The view took strange hold of her. Delicate wind cut through the delicate scent of blossoms and the city became a maze of glitter and hope. A feeling of comfort surrounded her, as if she could dive right into the streaming glow and fly in the air.

Then the comfort turned to rage. The rage wasn't against Walter or Judy, Jim or Rod, or even her mother for believing Mother of Mischief could win a woman praise and love. The rage was against herself. It grew like a baby inside her, seething and shivering, until she felt as if she really would fall over the edge of the summit. She stumbled to the car, holding on to the hood, still warm from the climb.

"Liar, liar, lying to yourself!" she screamed into the darkness.

She opened the car door and the light popped on. She caught a glimpse of herself on the windshield. She knew she was looking into the face of a fool. How willingly she had become responsible for those who transformed life into mischief instead of going out and transforming life herself!

She sat in the car, her hands grasping the steering wheel. All at once, her rage dissipated in the quiet car as it rocked a little from the wind. She remembered one day when she was a child how her father had come home from work. It was before Roosevelt's New Deal, and the Depression had hit the town of Rawlins hard. He sagged and complained, as when he went that morning to the shop, he found the window broken and some of the cigar boxes empty. Her mother had put her hands on his shoulders and said, "What's the good of blame and anger, George? Poverty eats away at one's dignity enough."

Mary saw that she had been poor — poor in her own mind and reasoning. She had been poor in the will to be one with her life. It had eaten away at her dignity. Blame and anger would not restore it.

She would remember that night years later. It was then she let go of her anxious eye, her stiff hip and her protruding ankle. It was then she vowed she would never be Mother of Mischief again.

~~~~~

She stayed in the car for a long time, feeling at one with the city lights and the wind rocking her gently back and forth. Dawn was beginning to show its face when she pulled into the driveway.

Walter was in the living room. He had no pipe and no paper. He was dressed in a dark suit and a dark hat. His head was bowed forward as if he were half asleep.

Mary let out a short laugh. "You look like you're at a funeral."

"Where have you been?"

She put her purse down on the hall table. "It's not your concern anymore, Walter."

"Don't talk like that, Mary."

"I suppose it's befitting." She nodded toward him. "In a way, we're both attending a funeral. The death of a marriage."

"Don't talk like that," he repeated.

"It's about time I said *something*, isn't it?" She leaned against the hall table. "You'll have your divorce, Walter. But I won't be taking the house."

He arched his eyebrows.

"I suppose it's for lawyers to discuss now," she said. "If you want to keep it, give me half the money. I'll need it."

"I told you, I'm taking care of you," he ventured.

"I'm taking care of myself," she said. "I'm going to San Francisco. College, possibly. I don't know yet." She turned away from him and shed her gloves and her coat.
~~~~~

"You're being very decent about this, Mary," he said.

"Do you realize, Walter," she murmured without turning around, "that I'm twenty-eight? Twenty-eight and my life is a blank slate. Your Judy will be twenty-eight in ten years. Maybe she'll be a blank slate then or maybe she'll be Mother of Mischief." She turned around and looked him straight in the eye. "I hope not. Mother of Mischief is where life ends and I wouldn't wish that on any woman."

She wandered up the stairs, leaving him with gaping eyes.

SOUL DESTINATIONS

The sleek red and orange locomotive glared back at the other trains standing like angry bullets in the morning sun of Los Angeles's Union Station.

"The most beautiful train in the world!" Joan murmured.

Her mother pulled the scarf closer around her small, wrinkled face. "Windy here. What did you say?"

"Nothing." Joan grasped the heavy suitcase firmly by the handle. "What time does the Daylight leave?" she asked a man in uniform who passed by.

"Where to, ma'am?"

"San Francisco, of course," Barbara answered with the snappishness she reserved for waiters, porters, and taxi drivers.

"Eight-fifteen on the dot, ma'am," the man murmured.

"They say it's the most famous locomotive in the country." Joan felt her eyes shine as she stared at it. "Number 4449."

Her mother shrugged. "It's just a number." She pulled her coat tighter around her small shoulders. "Did you buy a winter coat when you went splurging on all those new clothes? I hear it's cold up there in San Francisco."

"Do you know I had a dream last night?" Joan asked. "About that locomotive."

"You're always having crazy dreams." Her mother sniffed.

"I suppose everyone dreams before they take the train for the first time." She gave a little chuckle. "I was standing at the station with waves of smoke around me. I could see the locomotive light gazing at me like a wise eye. The wheels were running up and down, up and down, and breathing —"

"Trains don't breathe," Barbara interrupted.

"This one did. I could hear it inhale and exhale. But it wasn't going anywhere." She looked at her mother with alarm. "The wheels were moving but the train wasn't going anywhere!"

"Dreams are all nonsense," her mother said. "I tried to tell you that when you were a child. You didn't believe it then, and you don't believe it now."

Joan stared at the blur of people passing by. "The whistle blew and steam shot out at me like a beckoning finger. I ran toward it, but something kept clawing at me like a desperate animal. The air smelled of roses."

"You can't smell anything in a dream," Barbara scoffed.

"I did," said her daughter. "When the steam cleared, I realized I made it to the train. When it started to move, it made me feel giddy."

"All the more reason you should have accepted George's offer to drive down to San Francisco with him," her mother said with satisfaction. "That dream was an omen, you know."

"I thought you said dreams are all nonsense."

"Well, sometimes they can be omens," she reasoned.

"It wasn't that kind of giddiness, Mom." Joan held down her hat to keep it from flying off in the wind.

"Oh? And just what kind of giddiness was it?"

"The kind you feel when you're going on an adventure," she murmured. "When you're being let out for the first time."

"Let out?"

"I imagine it's how a convict feels when he's been in prison and served his sentence. He gets on the bus to Los Angeles, the first time in years he's been on one. So he feels giddy."

Barbara's mouth was tight. "Are you saying I've kept you in prison for thirty-five years?"

"No, of course not," said Joan as kindly as she could.

"No, of course not!" Barbara mocked. "You were never good at fibbing, Joan. I could always tell when you were lying."

Joan looked at the great eye of the locomotive, trying to keep her own from showing tears. "The woman at the ticket window said the 4449 has been pulling trains for twenty-five years."

"Then it will probably break down before you even reach Santa Barbara."

"Oh, Mom, really!" Joan sighed. "They wouldn't be running it if it didn't work."

"It would be just like these railroad companies to take your money and give you a broken-down train," her mother grumbled. "I remember a story your Aunt Ethel told me of a train she took and getting stuck in the snow in some God-forsaken town in Iowa. The railroad didn't send anyone for three days!"

"Well, there's no snow from here to San Francisco." Joan laughed. "I expect I'll be all right."

"Naturally, you'll be all right." Her mother's lips pursed. "You'll be free, won't you? You'll be out of prison."

"I didn't mean it that way." Joan watched a sheet of newspaper lying on the ground dodge the hurrying feet of passengers.

"I must tell Mildred all about that dream of yours," Barbara continued. "It ought to make her see just how grateful you are that she's taken me into her house."

"I didn't mean —"

"And Dottie will know how relieved you are she consented to take this burden that's your mother off your hands!"

"I never said you were a burden," Joan said quietly. "And I never said I was in prison. Why do you always have to twist my words around, Mom?"

Her mother dug her fists into her hips. "Is this what you're going to do to Ethel? Treat her like she's a burden when she's been so generous to take you in and not ask for room and board?"

"She's not taking me in, Mom," Joan said in an even tone. "I'm going to nurse her, just like I nursed Grandma and Grandpa. Just like I've been nursing you."

"Did I ask for a heart condition?" Barbara growled. "Did I ask for high blood pressure?"

"Please, Mom." Joan laid her hand on her mother's wrist. "Let's not fight before I'm about to get on the train."

"I expect you to be nice to Ethel." Barbara said. "You *need* to be nice to her."

"Why do I need to be nice to her?" Joan dug into her suitcase for her coat.

"You need to do everything she asks without groaning or complaining," her mother continued as if she hadn't heard. "And don't hide in your room after dinner with those travel books of yours. You need to be agreeable and accessible to her all the time."

"Why do I need to be agreeable and accessible?" Joan echoed.

Her mother's eyes shone like stars. "Because, my precious, you're not getting any younger. You've never been a raving beauty to begin with and now, at your age, you'll never find a man to take care of you."

Joan stiffened. "I don't know about that."

"*I* know," Barbara said. "Even pretty girls aren't always guaranteed a husband for life. Look at me. I was Citrus Queen of 1918, and I had all the men around me like bees to honey. And I still ended up with no security."

"Dad didn't do too badly by you," Joan pointed out. "He left you all that insurance."

"And you know just what he wanted me to do with it," Barbara snorted. "'Travel around the world with a wife and baby.' Pfft!"

Joan appealed to her with large gray eyes. "Don't you ever wish you had, Mom?"

"No!" The answer came with the force of a whistle from an incoming train. "I had better things to do than waste my time traveling around the world. I didn't need an old locomotive to take me out of prison!"

Joan flinched. "You want me to play up to Aunt Ethel. Is that it?"

"You're catching on." Her mother's voice was sour.

"You always talk as if we're mercenary."

"It's not a question of being mercenary," Barbara reasoned. "I've always been Ethel's favorite niece. She liked you when you were a child. She's got no one to leave all that money to. Why shouldn't it be you?"

"What's the matter, Mom?" Joan eyed her. "Afraid I'll be left destitute without a husband, and you'll have to provide for me?"

"I've *been* providing for you since you were a child!" Barbara straightened her tiny figure as two women passed them. "Now it's time you gave a little back." She cleared her throat. "And you have an obligation to Ethel. She's the only family I've got."

"I know," Joan murmured.

"Well, why shouldn't you save your aunt a little money and find yourself a good situation at the same time?" her mother snapped.

"I wasn't aware I needed a 'good situation.'"

"Oh, I don't say Ethel can't be a stubborn old goat," Barbara continued. "I half believe she invited you to live with her only because she knew she could boss you around more easily than any hired nurse. And after I moved into Mildred's house, I'm sure she realized I wouldn't need you anymore, and you would need a good situation."

"Why do I need to find a 'good situation?'" Joan repeated.

"Every woman needs a good situation." Her mother shifted her scarf to one side after the wind had blown it across her face. "It ought to be marriage, but we know that's out of the question for you now."

"Why does any woman need to find a 'good situation'?" Joan asked. "I think finding a happy situation is much more important, don't you?"

"A good situation *is* a happy situation, silly girl," Barbara sneered. "You've always been a dreamer like your father."

"Dreams were all I had, Mom," she said softly.

"Dreams and extravagant clothes." Her mother reached into her crumpled purse for her cigarettes. "So many things you could have done with all that money you saved. And you buy clothes!"

"You've been harping on that for weeks now."

"It's waste, sheer waste!"

Joan said with a sigh, "I don't expect you to understand."

"How many times have I heard *that*?" Barbara demanded. "I don't abide by waste, and you know it. Women in my situation have to count their pennies very carefully."

"Women whose husbands have the audacity to die a year after they're married," Joan lamented. It was a sob story she had been hearing since she was old enough to understand about death.

"That's right." Her mother took the bait. "I was a young widow and mother. What did I know about money? What did I know about taking care of a child?"

"I'm sorry that happened to you, Mom." Joan said. "I'm sorry I was only a baby when Dad died."

"Do you think I'm complaining about *that*?" Barbara gave her the narrow look of a wounded bird. "True, I was all alone, but I kept my chin up, as they say."

"You weren't exactly alone," Joan reminded her. "Grandma and Grandpa were living with us."

"And don't think *that* wasn't trying on my nerves either," her mother said. "Always criticizing, always needling about every little thing."

"I know," Joan said. "I took care of them when they got sick, remember?"

"You were only doing your duty," Barbara said. "You were always good at doing your duty, Joan." Although the words were warm, the tone was not. She said it as if she were dropping coins inside a slot machine. "You'll do your duty to Ethel. I have no doubt about that."

"Obligation and duty," Joan said. "You know, I think those are the two most frightening words in the English language."

"More nonsense." Barbara lit a cigarette. "You really should have gone with George, you know."

"To save money?" Joan eyed her.

"Well, not just that," she said. "Mildred told me George has always been sweet on you."

"Oh, really, Mom!" She looked away.

"I know you always turned your nose up at him because he's so devoted to Mildred, and he wears polka-dot bow ties," her mother continued. "But look at the proof. He's never married. He came to you himself to offer to take you to San Francisco with him."

"George is a nice man," said Joan. "But I have no interest in riding in a car with him all the way to San Francisco. I wanted to make this trip by train, alone."

"I don't understand why you didn't want to save your money by going with George." Her mother sighed. "You'll need money when you get to Ethel's, you know."

"I tried to explain to you why." Joan cupped one hand in the other. "Last night, I tried to explain. And just now, when I told you about the dream."

"Why, I wouldn't be surprised if even a plane would have cost you less than what you paid for that parlor car ticket, and you would have gotten to San Francisco in just a few hours!"

"You know that's not true," Joan said. "Anyway, you just said you wanted me to go with George in his car." She tried to hold back a smile, as her mother's contradictions were beginning to amuse her.

"It's foolishness, just plain foolishness!" Barbara finally lost her temper, her voice echoing over the screech of the brakes of a train that was just pulling out in the other direction. A few people standing near them, arranging their luggage on a cart, glanced at her.

Joan watched the smoke spurt around the figures that passed her. She could still see the silver light of the 4449 through the milky white curdles. It looked as if it were watching her. "Time and money aren't always the most important things in life, Mom."

"Only someone who can afford to squander both would say that," Barbara flashed. "We can't afford to do either. Not that you would think so, the way you bought all those smart clothes."

"I haven't bought new clothes since I graduated high school," Joan said.

"You don't need them," Barbara said. "Where you're going, no one will give a hoot how you look. Lucky for you."

"Since I'm no raving beauty?" Her mother had pointed out so often her plain, square face, her long limbs, and her pasty skin that she felt almost like a caricature now.

There was a call for the Ninety-Three to San Francisco leaving the platform in fifteen minutes. Joan felt her heart race. She held her hand out to her mother. "May I try to explain it to you again, Mom?"

"I'm not stopping you." Barbara shrugged.

"You know how much I've talked about traveling the world."

"Ever since you were a little girl."

"But I've never been out of Chestnut Street. The most I've ever traveled is today, here to the train station in Los Angeles."

"I've always given you everything you needed, haven't I?" Her mother's voice was cross and tired. "I don't see you needed to go looking for it anywhere else."

Joan's shoulders sagged with the weight of the heavy bag she still held in her hand. "It's not about that, Mom. It's about getting out of your own skin. You're born in one skin but you can wither inside of it, bones and all, if you don't get out and see things."

Her mother flinched. "You've always had a morbid imagination, Joan."

"Do you really find travel so objectionable?"

"I don't approve of wasting money on travel when there are other important things on which you can spend your money."

"Such as?"

"A television set, for instance."

Joan stared at her. "You always said radio was livelier and had better programs."

"Well, don't think I haven't wanted one." Barbara's shoulders stiffened. "I'm thankful Mildred has one of those new RCA models with the color screens."

Joan blinked from the cigar smoke that a man rushing past them blew in her face. "You never spoke of it before."

"I didn't think you wanted one, buried in your books all the time."

"I would have been delighted to have a television set for your sake," Joan said kindly.

Her mother rolled her eyes. "*Now* you tell me!"

"Every new thing is like a new experience," said Joan. "Don't you think everyone should have new experiences, Mom?"

"When you're nineteen, maybe." Barbara glanced at her. "When you're young. Not when you're thirty-five and not getting any younger."

"All aboard for the Ninety-Three!" The call sounded through

the station. Joan picked up her suitcase and motioned to the porter. "You've already said that this morning. Several times."

The call seemed to throw her mother into a panic. Her voice lost its edge and became almost girlish. "Honey, won't you change your mind and return that train ticket and go with George in his car?"

"Even if I wanted to, I couldn't now," she said. "George left last night."

"No, he didn't," said her mother. "He's leaving tonight."

Joan blinked at her. "But he said at dinner on Sunday he was leaving on Tuesday."

For the first time in a long time, her mother looked a little embarrassed. She scraped the dusty floor lightly with the left toe of her shoe. "Mildred and I persuaded him to delay his trip."

"You didn't!"

"It didn't matter to him whether he went on Tuesday or Wednesday," Barbara insisted. "And, well, I said I could probably get you to change your mind, and he was willing to wait for you."

Joan had never had much of a temper, but now she felt her arms and limbs grow as heated as her face, as if her entire body had been submerged in hot oil. "That was cruel of you. Both to George and to me."

"Cruel!" Her mother glared at her. "To give George the company of a girl whom he's always admired? To save you money and time? And you call your mother cruel for that?"

"You keep saying the same things over and over again." Joan now felt more wary than angry. "You know you're repeating yourself, Mom?"

"Giving up your last chance for a husband. Wasting time and money." Her mother's entire figure shot up like an arrow. "All for a silly whim."

Joan grasped her purse as the porter arrived with the Daylight cart and put her luggage onto it. She glanced down at the imitation Kelly bag she had bought along with the new clothes. Its envelope shape and loop handles were large enough to fit two books and cost only a tenth of the original. Yet, the way her mother couldn't stop rolling her narrowed eyes made clear she considered it a silly whim too.

"I must go." Her hands dampened inside her gloves. "Please, Mom, let's not part on a quarrel. I'll write you when I get to Aunt Ethel's."

"Well, don't write asking for money!" Barbara was shouting now over the noise of rushing feet. "If you squandered your savings on trifles, that's your business, but don't expect to come to me for a penny. My responsibility is finished. It's Ethel's turn now."

Joan grasped the handles of her new purse so hard, she felt the leather seam dig into her palm. "Goodbye, Mom." She leaned forward to kiss her but Barbara turned away, her hands folded in front of her. As Joan hurried toward the porter, she glanced back once. Her mother had turned around now, but she had put on a pair of large sunglasses that hid her expression. All Joan could see was her grainy face and firm lips, pursed like a button sewn too tightly to a blouse.

As she stood with the other passengers waiting to board the Ninety-Three, the wind rushed forward and wrapped white smoke around her, holding her up like the arms of a warm giant.

The porter was grinning at her, his teeth straight and white like pearls. "Ain't always easy leavin' the loved ones behind, is it, miss?"

Joan smiled at him. "Sometimes you wish it would be harder."

The man's laugh was deep and wide. "Ain't it the truth, miss. Ain't it the truth."

She felt embarrassed as she watched him struggle to raise the heavy bag through the narrow entranceway of the parlor car.

"Might have to put this in the baggage car, miss," he said.

"Oh, I couldn't do that!" When he looked at her quizzically, she said in apologetically, "All my books are there. I'll have nothing to do on the train."

As the porter tried again to lift the bag while she stood on top to help pull it up, long arms reached behind her and large hands grabbed it. A man with a blond flattop lifted it over his head and laid it down on the car floor.

"Thank you." She smiled at him, noting his boyish features did not hide the wings of a few wrinkles beginning around his eyes.

He did not smile back, but nodded and put his hat back on, which he had taken off to fit into the narrow entranceway. His angular face, pale lips, and gray eyes told of past exuberance, but as he moved swiftly to the back of the car and out the sliding door, she was struck by the way those lively features had now fallen in shadows.

~~~~~

She learned more about the man with the flattop hair by accident soon after she settled herself into one of the blue chairs in the parlor-observation car. A woman with curly gray hair and eyes close together in the seat opposite her began to chatter right away.

"All alone, dearie?" Joan nodded. "Well, we can't have that, can we?" She threw a glance at the young woman sitting next to her who had the same eyes. She stuck out her hand. "Beatrice Graham. My granddaughter, Carla."

Joan greeted both of them and was rewarded with a brisk, "Call us Bea and Carla. We don't stand on ceremony, do we, love?" Her granddaughter gave Joan a pleasant smile. Joan decided she liked them, though Bea seemed too anxious to gossip as she laid her knitting in her lap. Joan put aside her magazine, the smiling faces of the families in the pages glaring up at her like glossy reminders of what she had missed in her mother's parting. Bea seemed to take this as a cue and began a whirlwind of chitchat that hopped from one subject to another, sometimes in mid-sentence.
~~~~~

"You like traveling, dearie?" Bea asked.

"This is my first time," Joan admitted. "But I know I'm going to love it."

"Ought to have a friend with you." She lifted her finger at Joan. "Ain't right, a woman traveling alone."

"I like to be alone," Joan murmured.

"It ain't safe."

"I'm sure Joan can take care of herself, Gran," Carla said.

"We're going to San Francisco to visit with my best friend and see the fine arts school," she said. "Carla's thinking of becoming a designer. Ain't she got the classiest taste in clothes?" She looked approvingly at her granddaughter, who did indeed look chic and, subsequently, older than many college-aged girls Joan had seen. "Don't know about all this artsy stuff, but she seems to like it."

"You'll come to appreciate it, Gran." Carla didn't look put out in the least.

"I think those beatnik types get a little crazy in the head." She leaned forward and her voice lowered. "You saw Gary Colt on this train with that awful haircut."

"Who?" Joan asked.

"Colt," repeated Bea. "The famous violinist. Been all over the world, they say. Breaking strings at almost every concert." She chuckled.

"All over the world," Joan repeated.

"Course, he's no longer all that young." She cocked her head. "Forty or thereabouts, I'd say."

"Oh?"

"You saw him." Bea insisted. "I was just lookin' up when he came and helped you with that bag of yours." She glanced at the baggage rack above their heads where Joan had stored her books. "What you got in there, anyway?"

"Gran, really!" Carla scolded "You don't ask strangers those kinds of questions."

"Well, I guess Joan ain't a stranger, since we've been properly introduced." The woman sniffed, shaking the glasses perched on the edge of her nose.

"This man, Gary Colt," Joan said. "He was very nice."

"Nice, nothing." Bea sniffed again. "But he's talented. Child prodigy and all that. He played Carnegie Hall when he was just twelve."

"And he was invited back at fifteen," Carla continued the thread, clearly as familiar and fascinated by the story as her grandmother. "They say he played with such a passion he broke a string once during his performance."

"And wasn't invited back?" Joan guessed.

"Oh, no!" Bea put her knitting down. "He made a show of breaking strings after that. They call that entertainment. I call it crazy."

"It's a novelty, Gran, you must admit," Carla said.

"You mean it *was* a novelty," said her grandmother. "Don't forget what happened last year."

Carla sighed. "Too bad Mr. Colt's became a bit of a sinker."

"What do you mean?" asked Joan.

"The newspapers said people just started walking out of the concert." Bea leaned forward. "He was playing some Beethoven thing, and they walked out. Guess he wasn't breaking any strings that night." She chuckled.

"We saw a concert of his a few years ago," Carla added as she picked up a newspaper lying on the empty seat next to her. "Nothing wrong with it. But nothing right either, if you know what I mean."

"Well, I don't aim to waste my money like that." Bea stuffed her knitting in her basket. "Come on, honey. Let's play a few games of rummy before someone takes over the card table." She dug into her basket and came up with a deck of cards. "You play rummy, Joan?"

"I've played bridge quite a lot." She remembered with grated nerves the way her mother always dragged her as her partner when they played with Mildred and Dottie. "I'm not much for card games."

"We'll teach you rummy, then." The woman smiled.

Joan rose. "That's very kind of you, but I'm feeling a little shaky. I think I'll take a little walk."

"Be careful not to catch cold," warned Bea as she heaved herself out of the chair with the help of Carla's hand. "Those vestibules can be drafty."

She filed out after them as they made their way to the front of the car and saw to it that they were settled at the card table. Then, she slid open the train door and stepped into the vestibule. The queasiness she felt whisked away in that cool area of the platform. She closed her eyes and breathed in the magnificent air. She slid open the door of the adjoining car, passed the women's restroom, and leaned against the mural wall. A few people glanced up at the intruder but seemed content to go on with their reading or staring out the window.

As she turned to go back into her own car, she caught sight of Gary Colt standing away from the bulkhead. He presented a picture profile with his T-figured torso and his long legs and arms that fit comfortably in the crisp gray suit. He seemed more the continental type than a man who was "a sinker." And yet, even from that distance, she could see melancholy weighed his clean features as he looked into the parlor car, blinking at the light from the open curtains and blinds. He slipped back behind the bulkhead without speaking to anyone, and Joan had the impression he hadn't really seen anything. A pang of sadness entered her heart as she returned to her own car.

~~~~~

Gary sat back in the tweed chair, one hand dangling a cigarette he had barely touched and the other curled into a fist. His jaw was wired tight, and his eyes blurred to the view rolling past the window of the private drawing room. He had always been the watcher without seeing what he was watching. *Some-*
~~~~~

one's always watching you, son, so you have to watch them first, his father had been telling him since he was a child. It occurred to him that, even then, his father knew about the "someone" of his nightmares. *He's a demon, a devil, don't you let him destroy you, son. Don't you let him. You catch him watching you before he catches you watching him!* Now at Borden Manor, his father was still trying to catch those watching him before they caught him. Except they were not demons, but nurses, doctors, and orderlies.

It seemed impossible that only yesterday he had seen his father languishing on the lawn where the grass grew over rainbow flowers, and the scent of its fresh cut was stronger than the scent of the sea. Gary had gnawed the knuckles of his thumbs until they were raw and red the night before the visit, thinking of how his father would look — unkept, and wild-eyed in a dirty robe. He was relieved they let his father put on a decent jacket and trousers and had combed his hair back from his face the way he liked. He looked ready to step out to dinner at Romanoff's. The only thing that betrayed the condition the doctors called "dementia praecox" was the way his father's hands fell to his side, his fingers curling inward like claws as if he were ready to rake someone's face.

He had come to tell his father he was quitting music for good. He rattled on for twenty minutes while his father sat staring at the roses, his long arms draped on either side of his thighs, his hands clawing.

"I'll be forty this year, Papa," Gary said, continuously clearing his throat. "That's — ahem — middle age already — ahem — and no time to be traipsing around the globe. I want — ahem — to settle down, maybe even — ahem — find a wife and have a kid."

His father had looked up. Gary could see from the way his eyes drooped that he hadn't slept in days. "Kid?"

"Yes, Papa," he said. "You might be a grandfather someday." He tried to grin, but his lips felt like wood.

His father went back to staring at the roses. "Did I tell you Lucas has two faces, like Janus?"

"You don't have to worry about Lucas anymore," Gary said firmly. "They locked the gates on him here."

"He can split in two," his father continued. "Three, even. One part will make deviltry for the father, one for the son, one for the grandson."

"I told you — ahem — you don't have to worry about Lucas anymore, Papa. He's out of our lives for good."

"He's the reason." His father's voice rose. "He made those Russians turn on our people. He made our Greek and Russian friends turn against us and kill, kill, kill!"

"Papa," Gary spoke in a sedate tone, "that was in 1905."

"Lucas turns everything into decay. Roses, grass, love, talent." His father looked at him with ragged eyes. "You know he's the reason your career has gone to pot. *You* know, don't you?"

"You don't have to worry about him anymore," Gary said. "I give you my word."

His father's lips stiffened like iron. "If I ever get my hands on you, Lucas —" Suddenly he sprang up, his arms jerking up like a marionette's. "If I ever catch up with you, you devil, I'll —"

A nurse rushed out and calmed him enough to take him back inside. She threw a kind smile at Gary and murmured, "Dr. Willis would like to see you before you go, Mr. Colt."

Gary remained near the roses for a little while longer, watching a butterfly slide from one flower to another. In the serenity of the garden, he feared if he opened his mouth to speak, he would choke to death.

He found the men's room with a fountain outside. The long gulps of lukewarm water calmed him and wet his throat again. He knew the way to Dr. Willis' office by heart.

The man was brief. "It's a common thing with musicians, Mr. Colt. Their brilliance often ends up overriding their reason."

"My father was never a musician, not really," Gary lamented.

"He came from Russia, you see. His family fled the Pogrom riots in Odessa —"

"Yes, we know all about that," the man interrupted.

"My grandfather couldn't stop looking over his shoulder, even when they were living among their own in America," Gary droned on. "I remember how he used to put crumpled newspaper under the window so if someone tried to sneak in, he would hear them trampling all over the papers."

"Tragic." The doctor shook his head. "But I meant your father has the *temperament* of a musician."

"Do you think I'll go insane too?" Gary squeezed his hands together, feeling the sting of the raw knuckles.

"Certainly not." The doctor was sincere. "Dementia praecox isn't necessarily hereditary."

"And my father," said Gary. "Will he be this way forever?"

The man leaned back, forming a V with the lacing of his hands. Gary recognized this as his way of buying time while he came up with a judicious response. "It's hard to tell with patients such as your father. He might be melancholic for days, weeks, even years. And then, one day, he may snap out of it, just like that. Hard to tell."

"So you can't give me an answer?" Gary looked at the owl face with the oversized glasses that made the man's eyes look seedy.

"No responsible doctor could," said Dr. Willis.

Gary leaned forward. "I'm afraid I can't accept that."

"You'll have to." The doctor's smile was a little condescending. "We're doing all we can, of course. We've had some promising results with patients like your father giving them electroshock treatment."

Gary's chest went cold. "I read about that in the *Saturday Evening Post* last month."

"Oh, those articles were about a state institution, Mr. Colt." The doctor was still smiling. "We're not like *that*."

Gary rose. "Have you heard of the Feinstein Institute?"

The man sniffed. "Naturally. I believe they're doing some experimentation with, erm, holistic methods."

"I'm taking the train to San Francisco tomorrow morning," he said. "I plan on paying them a visit."

"Well, naturally, if you'd like a second opinion —"

"This is more than a second opinion," Gary said. "It might mean my father's life."

"Your father is in no danger of dying, I assure you."

Gary chuckled then, slipped into his coat. "I didn't think he was."

The train entered a tunnel. The darkness left him with a heavy feeling of what the doctor had told him, and he couldn't help but smirk. Speaking to Dr. Willis, he realized for the first time what an idiot the man was, a scientist who compartmentalized people and considered it adequate to sustain life rather than restore it. He had taken what Gary told him about his father and formed his diagnosis, prognosis, and treatment in what the *Post* articles had labeled "custodial." Gary blamed himself for having been so open, telling the doctor how his father's family had always been musical, how his great-grandfather had been a musician in Odessa, and his grandfather had taught his father to play. He also told him how the persecutions, the blood, the filthy ship to America and the inspecting hands of Ellis Island officials killed any desire his father ever had to play.

Gary stared at the reflection of his own face in the window. Dr. Willis called his father melancholic. Little did he know melancholy was just what his father had forced him to protest in his music. He had insisted Gary close the lid on despair as one closed the lid of a coffin before burial. His father pushed him to learn all those tunes that "flow into people and make them exuberant" — Vivaldi, Mozart, Rossini. *That's it, make the bow dance across the strings! Dance, dance, dance!* And his father had danced, laughing as Gary joyously tore the bow across the strings. Now that man who taught him to wrench joy out of a violin stared back at him through the dark window with empty eyes. That man he had left behind clawing at nothing and ranting threats against a phantom.

Gary's breath grew heavy. He looked out the window and realized sunlight was cracking through the glass. The train was out of the tunnel. He was all right now in the nicotine-scented room.

For the first time in months, he felt calm. He would stop giving concerts and stay in San Francisco where he intended his father to enter the Feinstein Institute, or some other humane place nearby. His father needed him now.

He thought of how many years his vibrancy had been swept up in trains like this one, rolling through cities in America and Europe in the dark with only a light flashing against bumpy stones, meeting bland faces at lonely stations. Now his father would find life again outside the nightmare his phantom Lucas had made of it, and Gary would have a chance to find life as well.

~~~~~

At lunch, Joan sat with Beatrice and Carla in the diner car. The oblong tables were covered with white tablecloths and voices rang softly through the small compartment. The surroundings were pleasant compared to the virtual silence with which she and her mother had taken their meals or the cawing voices of Mildred and Dottie at Mildred's dinners. But the strip of light in the center of the domed ceiling glared down at her with merciless enthusiasm, and the plaid carpet made her head feel heavy.

Bea noticed this and snapped open her purse, taking out a small bottle. "Ginger pills, dear. Good for motion sickness."

"It isn't that," Joan said. "I think the excitement of being here has just been a little too much."

"Lord, there ain't much to trains once you get used to them," said the old woman. "We do it all the time, don't we, love?" She gave her granddaughter an affectionate glance.
~~~~~

"But this is Joan's first trip, Gran." The young woman studied the menu card. "I remember the first train I took. I felt dizzy too."

"Well, you just gotta take a lot more train trips, then," said Bea in a hearty voice.

"I intend to." Joan smiled.

The Grahams got into an argument about whether the sirloin or tenderloin steak was best, and whether the steak would go better with the salad or grilled asparagus. Joan glanced out the window at the mountains in the distance, then turned her head to survey the dining car. Gary Colt was stepping in, loosely dressed in a tan sports coat and pleated blue pants. His face lapsed into a relaxed pose, and he looked more cheerful than when she had first seen him. He glanced left and right, and she half-rose, almost intending to offer him the fourth chair at their table. But his eyes fell on an empty table near the door where he took his place and studied the menu card.

"You look like a jack rabbit about to spring out of the road," Bea said with a laugh.

"Mr. Colt is here." She nodded toward the back of the car.

The woman eyed him. "He ain't nothing to get excited about, honey. It's not as if he's some sort of celebrity."

"He's no Elvis Presley," Carla agreed.

"Oh, Elvis!" her grandmother scoffed.

"Why, he hasn't even given a concert in over a year," her granddaughter continued.

"Well, he's been too busy tending to his father, hasn't he?" Bea scribbled on the meal check for both herself and Carla, handing it to the waiter. When the man left, she continued, not bothering to lower her voice, "They were saying in the *Times* last week his old man's in the looney bin and likely to stay there."

"Oh, Gran!" Carla sighed. "It's not his fault his father isn't quite right in the head."

"Listen, love, I'm a good deal older than you and Joan." She pointed the spoon she had used to stir her tea at each of them in turn. "One thing I've learned in all my years on this earth: Every one of us gets what's coming to us, one way or another."

"You mean God punishes the wicked and rewards the righteous?" Joan ventured.

"It ain't got nothing to do with God," the woman insisted. "We each of us do to ourselves."

Joan fingered the silver fork and began tapping it against the rim of her bread plate, gentle enough so that the faint scrape disappeared in the lull of the train. "Maybe you're right, Bea."

"'Course I'm right." The woman's chest puffed out. When the waiter set her plate down, she withdrew her rather bulky figure, sliding her chair back to make room for it.

"There was that reporter who wrote those articles about Gary Colt a few years back." Carla cut into her steak. "What was it he said about David Colt? 'The world's most ruthless and merciless stage father.'"

Joan felt her stomach churn as she picked at the cold cuts on her plate. "That's a little harsh, isn't it?"

"If the shoe fits —" Bea mumbled.

"Still, I feel sorry for him." Carla said. "The son, I mean."

"I don't!"

Joan gave at Bea a sharp look. The woman's eyes were pointed like a fox. "Why do you say that?"

"'Cause he's no better than the father, that's why!"

Carla leaned toward Joan and spoke in a low voice. "Gran thinks Gary as good as killed his college roommate."

"He did kill the poor boy!"

Carla lowered her voice even further. "Gran doesn't take a very compassionate view of things like murder."

"But how do you know it was murder?"

"I'm a bloodhound when it comes to reading the papers, dearie," said Bea. "Not much I miss."

Joan blinked at the corner table. The man's eyes were lifted toward the bar of light with alarming concentration. "He looks hardly capable of murder," she remarked.

"Oh, I'm not saying he took the gun to the boy's head," said Bea. "But murder ain't always direct, if you know what I mean."

"He went to the San Francisco School of Performing Arts, didn't he?" Carla asked.

Her grandmother nodded. "Take heed, love. They'll put you in fear of your life with their brutal competition if you don't watch out!"

"I don't intend to compete with anyone." Her granddaughter stiffened. "How about some of my potatoes, Gran? You like them on the Daylight." She dumped them in her grandmother's plate.

"But if Gary Colt is as talented as people say, why would he need to compete with anyone?" Joan asked.

"His looney father was behind it," said Bea. "Always making up contests for him and Mark — that was the roommate — instead of minding his own business!"

"That was hardly Gary's fault, was it?" Joan persisted.

"Maybe, but the newspaper said Gary Colt crossed any line drawn for him just 'cause he felt like it. He was ambitious then, not the feeble fly you see now."

"You just admitted his father was pushing him, Gran," Carla pointed out. "How heartless he must have been!" She pushed the empty dinner plate aside as the waiter set the berry parfait down in front of her. "He must have pushed and pushed Gary."

"He's a looney," Bea declared.

Joan's eyes slid to the table near the door. Gary's plate sat untouched in front of him. His eyes were still on the glowing bar. He looked almost as if he were praying, his fearful eyes asking for guidance.

"What did you mean when you said there are other ways of murdering someone that aren't direct?" she asked.

"Mark killed himself." Carla wiped her mouth with her linen napkin. "Shot himself. Poor boy."

"He was driven to it," Bea insisted. "Those who are pushed push others."

"Really, Gran, you might be more sympathetic."

"Gary found the body, didn't he?" Her voice hung cold in the heavy room. "The reporter said he found the body, told the college authorities, and was in the practice room with his violin a half hour later playing his heart out on some Mozart sonata. That's proof enough for me."

"That proves nothing," Carla argued.

Joan could no longer take their squabbling and excused herself with a headache. She ambled to the front of the dining car where Gary was seated. He suddenly rose and, still looking toward the strip of neon light, hurried out of the car. She glanced down at his table and saw he hadn't eaten a bite.

~~~~~

Later that afternoon, Gary sat on the couch in the drawing room with the blinds and curtains open, watching the train fly along the blue coastline. He lit a cigarette, a heavy brown one he rarely smoked because it filled the air with rancid mist. He wanted the smoke to fill his head and lungs. But even the cigarette couldn't keep the night of his last concert out of his mind.

He had come home to the lavish house in Newport Beach he had bought for himself and his father. How often his father said he felt safe in it! But he hadn't felt safe the night Gary walked in, haggard from the hurried flight back to Los Angeles, wanting to escape the memory of all the angry people who had walked out of the hall.

His father was sitting on the couch picking at the tassels on one of the pillows. Gary threw aside the starched jacket as he began telling his father all about the concert. His father had been what Dr. Willis called "stabilized" for some months, almost his old self, dancing to the fast bow as Gary had practiced for the concert. He expected his father to rail against the
~~~~~

ungrateful crowd, blame Gary's agent, reassure him he deserved better. But his father remained silent, and his hands were curled into claws.

"What's the matter, Papa?" Gary sank into a chair opposite him.

His father raised one of those hands. "I knew Lucas would be there to ruin everything!"

It was then Gary noticed the paper lying on the carpet. His father rarely read anything but the novels of Dostoevsky. Gary bent down and picked up a page separated from the rest. The headline was enough: *Aleksander Kaminski lost concerto found behind wall of old Kiev apartment.* The paper slipped from his fingers. "Oh, God!"

"There's no telling what Lucas will do," his father continued, his pale blue eyes nearly white.

He grasped the man's brittle shoulders. "Papa, have you been reading the letters? Have you?"

"Lucas works in mysterious ways." His father's voice trailed off. "Like Mephistopheles."

Gary's knees shook. "You *have* been reading the letters, haven't you?"

"Even one who spawns from a demon seed must have his moments of goodness," his father said.

"Goodness?" Gary covered his hand with his forehead. "A slaughtered man's concerto lying behind a wall. Yes, I suppose that's goodness, in a way."

"Lucas has his acts of kindness," his father lamented. "But what are they compared to his acts of evil?"

Mosquitoes buzzed above their heads, and Gary realized his father left the back door open. He slammed it shut, then said in a calm voice, "Lucas won't be bothering us anymore, Papa. Because I'm through."

"Through?" His father looked at him with ghost eyes.

"I won't ever perform again," he said. "I'll stay here in the city.

We have plenty of money. Lucas can't haunt us if there is no music, can he?"

His father was on his feet, glaring up at the small lights. The architect who built the house convinced Gary to let her put sunken lights all over the ceiling so the room shone with white spotlights glaring like little eyes. His father had always hated those bright lights. Bright lights, he told Gary, were what persecutors used on their victims.

For the first time in his life, Gary was frightened of his father. His face was savage and his gaze opaque and smooth. They were so different from the dark eyes that had watched him during rehearsals as a child. He couldn't convince himself those inverted eyes were a figment of his tired mind this time.

"You ought to be in bed, Papa." he reached his hand out.

His father's hands rose to the glaring eyes. The tight fists pounded into the air. His voice sounded almost foreign as he shouted, "I'll get you for this. D'you hear me, Lucas? You snuffed out one man's life, you won't snuff out another. I'll get you!"

The sea outside the train window flashed diamonds of light as the sun caught in the rolling waves. Gary's mind was also flashing. A flash of himself carrying his father to his bedroom amassed with gold and wood, and laying him down on the bed. A flash of the clock with hands at 2 a.m. And the most frightening flash of all: his father standing over him, his arms raised with the sword he bought from a retired samurai during a concert tour in Japan, holding it with both hands, and his eyes white while from his lips came the words, "Don't run away, Lucas. Your time has come."

By five o'clock, his father had been driven off to Borden Manor in Dr. Willis' car. No padded wagon, no big men in white suits, no straight jacket. nothing melodramatic about it. Dr. Willis had said, "We're taking a trip, David," and his father had answered, "I hope we see cows along the way."

Gary's eyes wandered to the black violin case lying on the

floor. He had not touched it since the night of the failed concert. The Klotz violin had been his grandfather's. As he opened the case and took it out, he felt the sleekness of its maple back and the silkiness of the strings. He reached into the velvet pocket of the case and felt for the music he had found when he was fifteen, not long after he broke a string from his violin for the first time in Carnegie Hall. The pages were still smooth but time had faded them a little. They looked almost as if they had been written on parchment.

The first time he had played the piece, his father came running into the room and had snatched it from the music stand. "Where did you get this?"

"In your suitcase, Papa," he said, all jubilance. "Why didn't you ever show it to me. It's wonderfully haunting."

His father's hand began to shake. "You shouldn't be playing it."

"Why not? I don't know the composer — Kaminski. Is he Russian?"

"Polish." His father's voice was quiet. "The tune is too maudlin and despondent for you."

"A little, maybe, but if I play it —"

His father howled, "It's the sort of tune they play when they bury people alive!"

"You exaggerate, Papa."

His father's shoulders relaxed, and his voice was calm when he said, "Trust me, my son. You would be courting disaster if you played that at one of your concerts."

"Why?" Gary blinked at him.

"People want something lively from you, like Vivaldi or Mozart," his father chuckled. "Even Daldoff with his falling stars and his love sickness are too maudlin for the likes of you." He laid his hand on Gary's shoulder. "Your music courts life, not death. Keep it that way."

It was only when he was packing his father's things for Borden Manor that Gary found the piece again. By then, he knew why his father hadn't burned it, and he couldn't bring himself to burn it either. He had no idea what possessed him to put it in his case. Perhaps it was the work of Lucas.

Over the quiet thumping the train wheels, he played. The old violin screeched out the tune in deep, echoing tones. Each note grew like a sniff, then a sob, then a gasp. He could see what his father had meant when he said the piece was for burying people alive. The notes flew out of the arms of a dream and into a nightmare.

~~~~~

The Grahams invited Joan for a game of rummy after lunch, but she declined. She made her way to the front of the car, sitting on the lounge chair nearest the door. She was aware beyond the porthole door lay the vestibule that led into the parlor car where she had seen Gary Colt.

She tried at first to read a book on the wonders of the Algarve, but her eyes kept lifting to that porthole. She closed the book and leaned back, trying to sleep. But her ears kept filling with the tones of a weeping tune weaving through a foggy night.

Her eyes snapped open. There *was* music coming from some-where on the train, real music. She glanced down the aisle, but the other passengers were either dozing or reading. She looked toward the porthole door and realized the sound came from the attached car. The strains of music were very faint, disappearing whenever the train leaned or bounced, but then came back again, following their own weeping melody. She recognized the sounds of a violin.

She entered the other car. The tune was still faint but closer now. Passengers were dozing, reading, or playing Solitaire. One man was doing some stretches, but he sat down again when she entered and turned his chair around to look out the window. No one seemed to be paying attention to the music.

Joan leaned against the partition, holding her hand to her forehead. Perhaps she was imagining it. Hearing the music of
~~~~~

strings because Gary Colt was a violinist and had been on her mind since he lifted her leather bag into the train. But, no, the sound was real. The song softly sobbing through the train car was real.

She crept down the aisle and reached the partition, where a round mirror glared back her own face with concern and wonder. The music was louder now.

Then the tune ended, and she heard a muffed, heavy sigh. Something that sounded like a suitcase opened and closed. She raised her hand to the knob, hesitating. But then the door slid open, and the boyish features of Gary Colt met her gaze.

"Oh, I beg your pardon!" She stepped back. Then, she blurted out, "You helped me with my bag this morning."

"I remember." He opened the door all the way.

"I don't want to disturb you," she mumbled.

"I feel like talking," he said. "And you look like a good listener." His tone was a little abrupt, but the sentiment was sincere.

She stepped into the drawing room. "I've been told I am." She put on the warm and disarming smile that made everyone trust her.

He flushed. "I'm sorry. When you're a child prodigy, you get feted and fawned over, so you just assume everyone wants to be with you."

"I'd rather people be direct," said Joan. "You're Gary Colt, aren't you?" He nodded. "I'm Joan Hornsby." His hand felt light and bony in hers. "You were playing that music, weren't you?"

He fiddled with a Zippo lighter but seemed reluctant to use it on the fresh cigarette in his hand. "I thought no one could hear a thing over the train noise."

"No one did," Joan said. "I was listening for it. I was hoping you might play."

"You've never attended one of my concerts, have you?" he asked, a little ruefully.

"No. I wish I had."

"If you had, you would know it's not the sort of tune that's part of my repertoire."

"What is your repertoire?" She looked at him evenly.

"Lively, bubbling pieces," he said. "Pieces that sing."

"Sing?"

"My father's word," he said. "He taught me that if I wanted to get anywhere as a violinist, I have to make people want to get out of their seats and dance. He used to dance while I played."

Her hand clasped the arms of the chair. "No one would dance to that tune."

"I know that," he said sharply. "My father once said it's a tune you play to bury the dead."

She leaned back. "I take it you didn't write it."

He cast his eye at the window. "A man named Aleksander Kaminski wrote it."

"I know that name!" She sat up. "Wasn't there something in the paper about him not long ago?"

He pressed his hands together. "He was a friend of my father's."

"What you played was hauntingly beautiful," she said. "What's the name of it?"

"I don't think Kaminski ever gave it a name," he said. "He didn't have time."

She blinked at him. "I remember now. The paper said he was killed in a concentration camp."

"He never played it," said Gary. "He sent it to my father in 1943."

The silence wrapped around her in the lighted room. "I shouldn't have said anything." She put her hands on her cheeks to keep him from seeing how inflamed they were from shame.

"I'm glad you did," he said. "We can't remember unless we form the words, can we?" He began to gnaw on his knuckle.

She watched him. "Did you ever meet him?"

He shook his head. "His family went back to Poland when he

was a boy. They didn't like it in America. Oh, why the hell didn't they come back when —"

She sighed and looked at the scenery. "It's hard to know when to leave if your soul is grounded in one place." She thought of the small ranch-style house where she had spent all her years, painted a sly yellow to make it look brighter than it really was. Then, she smiled at him. The long-practiced soft look that had unburdened her family of their woes seemed to unwind Gary. He started to talk, and the light dimmed inside the little drawing room.

"I'm glad he's not alive," he said. "If he were, if I met him on the street today — I would kill him myself."

"That's a rather violent thought," she remarked, but her gut tightened as she remembered her conversation in the dining room with Bea and Carla: *He's no better than the father.*

"If it weren't for him," said Gary. "If it weren't for his letters, my father would be — he wouldn't be where he is."

Joan turned to the window, remaining silent.

"There would have been no Borden Manor," he murmured. "There would have been no Lucas."

"Lucas?" she asked softly.

"A figment of my father's imagination, according to the doctors," Gary smirked. "A demon with two faces, according to my father. Three, even."

"I see."

"Have you ever seen Henry Fuseli's painting, *The Nightmare?*" Joan nodded. "That woolly demon sitting on the sleeping woman in white. That's Lucas, always crouched over someone with those hollow eyes and that twisted mouth."

"Was he your nightmare too?"

"When I was a child," he said. "I stopped believing in him a long time ago."

"Demons are only real when you believe in them." Joan nodded.

"No, it wasn't that," said Gary. "It was because I realized Lucas wasn't the demon. It was Aleksander Kaminski."

The afternoon sun hid behind clouds over the crowning cliffs showing in the distance. The train was so close to the edge, it looked as if they were skimming the waves. She suddenly saw inside the mirror reflection a man approaching middle age with the fire and ice of Dorian Gray at his most degenerated state.

A gasp rose from Gary's throat. "Was it Papa's fault my grandparents made a go of it in America and Kaminski's parents didn't?"

"Naturally not," Joan murmured.

"Was it Papa's fault they didn't think of leaving Poland before — before it was too late?" Gary's voice shook as his hand rested on his knee. "He kept writing to Papa letters about Poland and the Nazis. Papa always said he was a brilliant musician, seeing the details others missed. He used his talent for minutia all right — used it to destroy the only friend he had!"

"How bitter you are against a helpless man," Joan said.

"It wasn't fair." Gary rubbed his sore knuckle. "He gave his letters to musicians coming to the States and told them to hide them in the lining of their instrument cases so they wouldn't go through the censors, even though he knew the consequences if those musicians were caught." He looked at Joan with terrified eyes. "That wasn't fair, was it?"

"Maybe," she ventured, "he knew what his fate would eventually be, and he wanted one person in the world to know why."

He blinked. "You really believe that?"

She nodded. "Maybe he was fighting his own army of Lucases."

He looked at her for a long time, the startling glare leaving his eyes. "I never thought of it that way." He gave the reflection in the window a crooked smile. "He wanted to come to America again. But by then it was too late."

"How do you know it was too late?"

"He wrote Papa he was going to try and get to America. We never heard from him again."

They sat silent for a while. Then, Joan asked, "Why did you play Kaminski's piece just now?"

"I was thinking of so many things," he mused. "You can't help but let the train wheels drum into your head. It seemed the perfect dirge."

"For whom?"

"Two men," he said. "One dead in body but not in soul, one dead in soul but not in body."

"Aleksander Kaminski's the first," she said. "I know that. Won't you tell me who the second is?" She peered at him, aware the despair that had struck him that morning had now returned.

"My father," he said. "I'll be moving him to a place in San Francisco. Maybe they can bring back the dead." He let out a harsh laugh.

She stared out at the level water. "I know what that feels like, when you've become an empty shell someone else has taken over."

"But we don't have to stay dead, do we?" he asked. For the first time, she felt he was seeing her clearly, like a schoolboy looking to his teacher for guidance.

She held his gaze for some time, feeling the words absorb her like ink inside a handkerchief. She reached out her hand.

They were silent for a time, holding one another's hand. The dense view of the sea lent a dim to the room. The silence began to compress her, and she asked, "What will you do now? I mean, after you've settled in San Francisco."

"I really hadn't thought about it," he said lightly. "Maybe I'll buy a newspaper stand on Market Street or work on one of those fishing boats you always see docked in Fisherman's Wharf."

"You're giving up music, then?"

"Not much point in it if I'm not giving concerts."

"Oh, but you could do lots of other things," she insisted. "Compose, for example."

He gave her a sharp look. "Like Kaminski? Should I offer dirges for dead men to the public?"

"All right, then," she challenged. "How about teaching?"

He flinched. "I wouldn't want to watch little boys and girls go through the same cut-throat competition I did."

Joan remembered what Bea had said: *The world's most ruthless and merciless stage father.* "Then don't," she said. "Mentor them so they know they have someone on their side."

He stared at her. "Like a Big Brother of the music world?"

She smiled. At some point, she had taken hold of both his hands in hers. She looked down at them, realizing they were no longer the gnarled, troubled hands of a man in midlife but the hands of a boy, strong hands that could pluck a bow across the strings of a violin with passion.

She slipped her hands out of his and placed them in her pockets so he wouldn't see them shaking. The sea had disappeared behind curvy mountains. "Isn't it wonderful how you only have to travel on a railroad track to reach a new place, a new world, even?"

"It's not enough." His tone was brutal. "I've been on many train tracks to many new places and new worlds. It's like the living body and the living soul. One without the other kills them both."

She took a breath. "You mean your body can be in a different place, but if your soul is the same, you'll always be back where you started?"

"Something like that."

Her legs felt as fragile as matches as she left the drawing room and made her way back to the observation car. She saw Bea and Carla were dozing. She crept past the resting heads and softly snoring people to the observation section gathered like a cup at the end of the car. There was one oblong window staring into the vast space of mountain range and gray-blue sky. She watched while the train moved forward, leaving behind her dead soul.

~~~~~

The fury of disembarking the Daylight was something Joan would remember the rest of her life. Those people who had been drowsing or quietly contemplating life before the train pulled into San Francisco were now in a flurry of folding, finding, and chattering with strangers they would likely never see again. The Grahams disappeared and so did many of the faces that had become familiar to her over the nine-hour train ride. And yet, as Joan joined them in their gathering and flustering over what they would do next, she felt a part of something important, something that had new life.

She managed to lug the leather case with her books back to the entrance and, as she raised her hand to call for a porter, hoping this time to draw someone with a more muscular frame, she saw the familiar granite eyes and blond hair. Gary was smiling at her, a quiet, decisive smile. The sagging melancholy was gone, and he looked years younger.

As he lifted the bag to the platform, he mused, "A heavy burden you've had to endure all this time, isn't it?"

"On the contrary," she said, "it has the key to life for me."

He continued to smile, not asking her what she meant. "I decided to take your advice. I have a friend who I think might help me get started."

"I'm glad."

"Miss Hornsby — may I call you Joan? I feel as if I should. You call me Gary, of course."

"Yes."

"I hate these end-of-the-line goodbyes," he mused. "You feel like you've exposed yourself to people, locked for hours in those little cars, and then, it's as if it all disappears, like when you wake up from a dream."

"And you don't want the dream to end?" She blinked at him.
~~~~~

"I only meant — look, I'll be staying at the Hilltop Hotel. They have a decent restaurant there. I thought — " He looked down at the suitcase. "I thought we might have dinner together sometime."

She felt a blush escape her cheeks. "That's very kind of you."

"You haven't told me anything about yourself," he said. "I was the one doing all the talking."

"I'm used to it," she said. "Maybe I should start getting used to something else."

"You should." He suddenly took her hand. "I can be a good listener too."

"Well, thank you." She stepped down to the platform. "I won't forget the invitation."

"You'll be busy, I'm sure," he said, letting go of her hand.

She glanced at him. "Not too busy, I think."

She could feel his smile widening as she threaded her way around the rushing figures to look for her aunt.

She hadn't seen Aunt Ethel since she was fifteen, but she knew her right away. She expected to see her with the sallow skin and spotted neck of one who had settled into a long illness. Instead, she was surprised how little her aunt had changed. Though her hair was gray instead of brown, it still fell in a comfortable mane around her shoulders and, despite the grooves in her skin, it glowed like her lively eyes.

"Good to see a familiar face for a change." Aunt Ethel gave her a fierce embrace. "Seems like nothing but strangers around me all this time. Strange nurses, strange doctors, strange neighbors. This town is worse than New York City, and I lived in Manhattan for more years than I care to remember."

As her aunt drove the car through the traffic of Market Street, Joan cleared her throat and said, "I've got a shock for you, Auntie."

"In seventy-eight years, I've yet to find anything shocking, my dear." Her aunt chuckled.

"I'm going to travel around the world."

"Are you?"

"Oh, not right off, of course. I have lots to see before that. I don't even know my own country!"

"Neither do most people," said Aunt Ethel. "And your mother doesn't know anything beyond her own garden. Barbara was always the little mole."

"I don't want to be a mole." Joan realized how fierce she sounded as her voice echoed in the roomy Chevrolet. "I just don't want to be a dead soul."

"Eh?" Her aunt looked sharply at her.

"I mean to take care of you just as well as any nurse." Joan took a breath. "But I want to be paid like a nurse." She was clutching the loop handles of her purse.

"So." Aunt Ethel, now at the stoplight, turned to study her niece with complete abandonment. "You want to travel, and you expect me to finance you."

"I'm not asking for a handout." Joan stiffened. "I've taken care of people all my life. I know how to comfort lonely people, and I'm a good companion. I know when to call a doctor and when not to."

Her aunt laughed. "Well, that's better than any of the ninnies I've had who had the phone in their hand at the smallest sniffle. Worried about getting sued for negligence, I guess." Her face softened and she reached out to pat Joan's hand as the light turned green. "I wasn't objecting, my dear. I had opportunities to go abroad when I was your age and younger. And I took them, too."

"Naturally, I won't do anything until —" She bit her lip, not wanting to think of this aunt, whom she realized was still as spunky as ever, buried in some grave.

"Until I'm all bones?" The woman chucked again. "Well, I don't intend that to be for a while, and I don't intend for you to wait that long either. We can make arrangements later on once you're settled in and saved some money. Why, I might even go with you now and then." Her eyes sparkled like diamonds.

"I would be happy to take you along," said Joan. "But sometimes, I'll want to go alone."

Aunt Ethel nodded. "People ought to discover new places on their own."

"So your soul can be in the same place as your body," Joan murmured, looking out the window. She watched as the tall Victorian houses looked at her with sympathetic eyes.

DEVOTED

$\mathcal{R}$achel and Jack's engagement party was Rachel's party all the way. The decorations were pink, purple, and green in exactly the shades she loved. The living room furniture was moved into the den, and rented chairs bordered the room so as to leave a large, rectangular space free for dancing. Rachel begged her father for a live jazz band, but he shuddered at what the neighbors might say when they heard the blaring trumpets and banging bongos seeping through the worn walls of their priceless Victorian homes, so Rachel gave in to a more sedate ensemble.

That Saturday night was a clear one in Pacific Heights, the stars making a canopy of lights over the turrets and towers on the hills. Rachel insisted on formal dress, so her father Warren consented to a tuxedo. As he struggled with the bowtie, his eyes caught hold of the china pug on the bureau, the image of fields filled with burned wheat and yellow grass in its sad eyes. His lawyer mind, always making associations, saw his sister, whose face resembled the pug's almost in every detail. He called to Carol, "Do you think it was wise to invite Amelia tonight?"

His wife gave him a funny look. "What do you mean?"

"Well, she's not exactly the life of the party," he said. "And she doesn't really fit in with the Phillips."

"I think she's as good as they are," Carol insisted. "Even if she isn't as socially or financially prosperous."

"It isn't that so much," said Warren. "You know how she's been since —"

"She *is* Rachel's godmother." Carol stepped into the gold lace dress, threading her arms into the straps. "We could hardly avoid it."

He threw another glance at the pug as he undid the bowtie and made another attempt to tie it. "I just hope she doesn't say anything crazy to Jack or his parents. It wouldn't do for them to think there was a looney in the family."

"Warren! Your sister is *not* a looney." Carol stood with her back to him, waiting for him to zip her up. "She's always been a little peculiar, even before the incident with Don."

"Peculiar," Warren snorted. He kissed his wife's bare shoulder. "You always have such an elegant way of putting things, honey."

"Every family has its eccentric relations." She shooed his hands away and did his tie up herself. "I imagine Rachel's already warned Jack and he, like the good boy he is, warned his parents."

"Warned Jack about what?" Rachel appeared in the doorway of her parents' bedroom. She was perfectly done up to look like the latest Channel model with her beaded, fitted dress and bobbed blond hair bubbled at the top. Her silver high-heeled pumps were swinging from two fingers in her dropped hand.

"Your mother was just commenting on your Aunt Amelia's 'peculiarities,'" said her father in a dry voice.

"Peculiarities?" Rachel laughed. "She's downright looney."

"That's exactly what I said!" He grinned at his wife and put his arm around his daughter.

"All great minds think alike, Daddy." Rachel winked.

"I think you're both being very unfeeling." Carol snapped the bracelet on her wrist.

"In other words, if we were mothers, we would understand." Warren winked at his daughter.

"I will be one of these days," Rachel reminded him.

"If you had to go through what she went through with Don —" Carol began.

"Just what exactly *did* she go through?" Rachel sat on the bed and slipped on the pumps. "Two years ago, her eighteen-year-old son decided to leave the nest. End of story."

"That is *not* the end of the story, and you know it, Rachel."

"Your witness, honey." Warren grinned at his daughter.

"When a child doesn't call or write his mother in two years," Carol's voice lowered as if children were hiding behind the curtain with watchful eyes, "it's only the beginning."

"It was her own fault, Mom." Rachel smoothed down her dress. "You know that."

Her mother paused with her lipstick poised, the swan dive of her mouth hard in the mirror. "If you call loving your child unconditionally a fault."

"Now *you're* not admitting there's more to the story," Rachel snapped. "She didn't just love him unconditionally. She hung a noose around his neck. And she kept pulling it tighter and tighter."

"Remember, Carol, our daughter has insider information," Warren said. "She was closer to Don than anybody."

"I was." Then, with the voice that her parents called "m'lady's command" ever since she was a child, she added, "Can we not talk about Don tonight?"

"Your aunt is bound to mention him."

"Well, then, I'll just remind her if *she* weren't here tonight, maybe *he* would be!"

"Now, honey, that's unfeeling," said her father in a firm voice.

"I'm sorry, Daddy," she said. "But Don and I promised to be at one another's engagement party, and now he's not here. We planned a huge party."

"I suppose the money I've spent on this shindig isn't huge enough for you?" Her father eyed her.

"She didn't mean that, Warren," Carol said.

"I just wish he were here." Rachel made a swift retreat to the living room.

"Sometimes your attempts to make light of a situation are out of place, Warren." Carol's eyes melted through the soft light. "You know they were like brother and sister."

Warren blinked at the empty doorway where his daughter had stood. "Poor kid. Imagine not having a brother at your wedding."

"He could always call," said his wife. "Maybe he saw the announcement in the society column. He might still —" Her husband gave her a heavy look.

~~~~~

In the living room, Rachel peeled back the curtain, exposing the perfect circle of light tying a knot around the enclosed street. Although their house was in a section less visible from downtown, it was exclusive and homey at the same time. She had always been comforted by the dead-end circle with the four houses latching into its rim so that even the earthquake four years ago hadn't made a shiver. She remembered thinking how, if the rumbling ground couldn't shake apart Coral Street, nothing could.

Essie, their maid, informed her that "Mr. Jack" had arrived. Rachel whirled around to confront the tall young man with the slightly tailored figure and dark, thin line of facial hair from his chin to his sideburns. She took in his cheerful eyes and smile and felt the comfort she was seeking wash over her like a wave. She was in his arms in a moment.

"Mom and Dad just got into the city an hour ago. They wanted me to come with them, but I said I promised you I'd be here early. Looks like everything's already arranged." Jack
~~~~~

glanced around the room. "Quite a spread your father's giving us."

"*He's* giving us?" She laughed. "It was all me, dearest, and you know it!"

"Whatever the princess wants, the princess gets." He bowed.

She fingered the beads of her skirt. "Why did you call me that?"

"What?"

"Princess."

"Oh, I didn't mean anything by it, sweet." He put his arm around her. "I know girls find that offensive nowadays, but every guy wants his fiancée to be a princess."

"I was Princess Scrabble once," she murmured.

"Scrabble?" He laughed. "I didn't know you were partial to the game."

"I used to be," she said. "Me and the Scrabble Knight played all the time."

"You can be kooky sometimes, Rachel." He took the scotch and soda Essie brought him.

"I suppose it was kooky," Rachel admitted. "That's how Don and I played sometimes."

"Hey, who's Don?" His eyes narrowed with playful jealousy.

"My cousin, you idiot!" She gave his arm a playful push.

"You never mentioned you had a cousin," he said. "You made me think you were a poor, little rich girl with no family. Other than your aunt, of course."

"Don was — is — was —" She took a few gulps.

"Which is it?"

"Don *is* my cousin," Rachel said in a firm voice, "Aunt Amelia's son."

"Good to know who I'll be meeting tonight," said Jack, smiling.

She stared into the empty fireplace. "We haven't heard from Don in two years."

He sat down beside her and slipped his arm around her waist. "I'm sorry, sweet. I shouldn't have asked."

"Aunt Amelia will be here, though."

He watched her. "You're not pleased."

"Should I be?"

"Well, she's the only aunt you've got, isn't she?"

"Sometimes, aunts can be like unwanted ghosts."

He sat up. "That's pretty harsh, don't you think?"

"Mom just accused me of being unfeeling," she said. "Maybe I am." She took his arm. "Maybe you would be too, if you knew what I knew about Don."

"What is it you know?" he asked. "Did Don get sent to Siberia or something?"

She felt her eyes grow misty. "He disappeared."

"What do you mean, disappeared?"

"He said he was going to see a friend up in Tahoe. He never showed up there."

Jack leaned forward. "How old was he?"

"Eighteen."

He shrugged. "Well, lots of kids go on the road these days. Finding themselves, or whatever they call it."

"Except they keep in touch with their families." Her voice was hard. "They send a postcard now and then. We haven't heard a word from Don."

"Maybe your Aunt Amelia got a postcard from him lately," he ventured.

"I'll ask her tonight," she said. "I'm sure she'll be glad to talk about Don. She loves playing the mama martyr." She put the glass down with an unsteady hand.

~~~~~

By the time the party was in full swing, Rachel had forgotten all about the painful conversation. The rowdy jubilance of her friends and Jack's overrode her solemnness. It was a small gathering with only her parents and Jack's as representatives of the
~~~~~

older generation. Rachel, who had been playing hostess at her own parties since she was a teenager, was in her element, strutting around like a proud goose, sharing martinis and deviled eggs as she laughed over some offhand comment, accepted congratulatory kisses, and referred to Jack as "my sweet husband-to-be" with the unhinged glee that was such a part of her nature. Everyone smiled as they watched the young couple. Even Jack's parents, an older and stuffier version of Rachel's, seemed willing to be observers rather than entertainers in the room full of young people.

"I see Aunt Amelia is late as usual," Rachel remarked to her mother.

"Maybe she wants to make an entrance," Jack's father said with a lopsided grin.

"You did say she was your godmother, didn't you, dear?" Mrs. Phillips asked.

"Yes, my godmother," answered Rachel.

"She's not the kind to make an entrance," said Carol. "Amelia is very modest."

Rachel's eyes slid toward Warren, and he rolled his toward the ceiling.

"What sort of person *is* Mrs. Grant, if I may ask?" Jack's mother shifted her matronly figure away from Essie as the maid passed by her with the tray of drinks. "She's been a bit of a mystery to us."

"There's no mystery about my sister." Warren grabbed a glass from Essie's tray, despite Carol's warning eye.

"Amelia is a very warm and kind person," Carol insisted. "Isn't she, Rachel?" Now the warning look was passed to her daughter.

"At times," Rachel said vaguely.

"She can also be clingy and unsophisticated at times," her father mumbled.

"Warren!"

"Well, it's true, dear," he said. "The Phillips' may as well know it now. Oh, she means well," he assured them. "But there's a reason why people take her to be twenty years younger than she really is."

"Don't be unfair, Dad." Rachel felt the retribution of her earlier brutality toward her aunt as she looked at Mrs. Phillips' raised eyebrows. "Aunt Amelia has always been sort of – well, living in her own world. Oh, not in a bad way. Just different."

"Amelia has her own way of seeing things," Warren agreed.

"I think I know what you mean," said Mr. Phillips. "Once I had a distant uncle who was like that. Used to talk about being in the Boar War, but he was never even in the army, much less the British army!" He laughed.

"It's not that, exactly," said Rachel. "Aunt Amelia doesn't make up stories about herself."

"She's just always been very involved with family, especially her son," said Warren. "Lived through him, you might say."

Mrs. Phillips smiled. "Most mothers do at one time or another, Warren." She threw an affectionate look at her own son.

"Yes, but with Amelia, it sometimes made her act funny and say funny things," said Rachel.

"What do you mean, funny?" Jack asked.

"Oh, I can't explain it." She set down her empty glass on one of the small tables that had been pushed aside with the chairs.

The doorbell broke into the conversation and silky music someone had put on the stereo while the band rested.

"That will be Aunt Amelia." Carol was suddenly alert, raising her hand to Essie, who was heading into the front hall. She gripped Rachel's arm. "I think you and I ought to let her in." In a lower tone, she added, "We don't know what kind of mood she's in, do we?"

Rachel, who had swiped a plate of pâté and crackers from one of the hired maids and was holding it high above her head on one palm to her friends like a waiter in jest, handed it to Jack and obeyed her mother.

Amelia looked her usual modest self in a dark blue dress and short jacket that molded her small figure gracefully. Rachel hadn't realized her aunt had lost so much of her girlish look, as her strawberry hair was now tainted with silver, and there were crow's feet around her eyes. She seemed to be taking in the elegantly coiffed hedges and perfectly placed flowers that, even under the porch lights, showed their glorious bright color.

"I've always been proud of how Warren's done so well for himself," she declared with her waxy smile as she looked around the front hall.

"The *Bay Area Business Times* recently put him on the list of the top fifty lawyers in the city." Carol took Amelia's arm and motioned for Rachel to take the other arm.

Amelia gave her a floating look. "You know, I used to send Donny to this house all those weekends hoping he would make Warren his mentor."

"Don had his own aspirations, Aunt Amelia." Rachel felt her nerves grow unsteady.

Her aunt gave her the same vacant look. "His own father had nothing to offer him but an unmarked grave buried in the Normandy American Cemetery, poor man."

Rachel caught her mother's arched eyebrows as she raised her head a little above Amelia's.

"Have you heard from Don?" Rachel ventured.

Her aunt's eyes slid to the oblong hall mirror. "Do you know, sometimes when I look in a mirror, I can't see my own reflection? Just lately, I can't see my own reflection."

"I see a lovely woman who still has the smile of a girl." Carol gave her hand a squeeze.

"I see Minnie Mouse," Rachel said.

"Rachel!" Her mother hissed.

Her aunt gave her a quick look. "Donny used to call me Minnie Mouse. He never told me why."

Rachel bit her lip. Don had told her why: *Mom's voice squeaks when she gets mad.* "I asked you if you heard from Don," she repeated, trying not to sound impatient.

"What? Oh, no, dear, I haven't. Have you?" She peered at her with clear blue eyes, the same color as Warren's.

"No, of course not," she said. "I would have told you if I had."

"Do you think maybe he's gotten involved with some strange group or something? There are so many bad people around, and so many children get confused when they're out in the world alone." She clutched Rachel's hand.

"Don't imagine things, Aunt Amelia," she said in a curt voice. "Don's not lost."

"You know that for sure?" Her aunt looked at her with wild eyes.

"Of course I know it!" She wretched her hand free. "And you should know it too."

"Rachel only meant Don's always been a sensible young man," said Carol.

"But these children —"

"He's not a child!" Rachel's voice echoed in the hallway. Then, composing herself, she said, "Come meet my fiancé, Aunt Amelia. He's going to be family soon."

She was disappointed her aunt wasn't more cordial when she made the introductions to Jack and his parents. It was the one thing she had always loved about Amelia. Don once said, "Mom's always welcoming, always warm. You can imagine her in the kitchen watching over a pot of stew or kneading bread or frosting a cake. She was born in a kitchen and in the kitchen she'll die!" But Aunt Amelia didn't have on her kitchen look tonight. Instead, her gaze fell on Jack's lower face. She was staring openly at him. Rachel could see both Jack and his parents were embarrassed.

"Aunt Amelia thinks you're handsome, Jack. That's why she can't take her eyes off of you." She took hold of his arm. Her eyes darted at her father, and she saw he also realized her aunt was mesmerized not by Jack's good looks but by something else.

Jack gave her his good-natured smile and took her hand. "I never told Rachel this, but I've had a few female clients stare at me. Completely harmless, of course."

"It's because you have the look of a young man who will help any old lady across the street." His father gave a heavy laugh. "Isn't that true, Mother?" His wife nodded with a quiet smile.

But in spite of their jesting, Rachel felt nervous as her aunt continued to stare at her fiancé with that look she got where her features settled like a frightened bird.

"How long did it take you?" The question shot out like a dart from her aunt's thin lips.

"I beg your pardon?" Jack blinked.

"How long did it take you to grow that beard?"

"Why, Aunt Amelia!" Rachel realized the reason for her aunt unfriendliness, why she stared. A sense of dread filled her.

His hand brushed his chin as he laughed. "I almost forgot it was there."

"How long?"

"I don't remember," he admitted.

"Don't you?" Her hand was still shaking in his.

"What an odd question," Rachel heard Mrs. Phillips murmur.

"Really, Amelia," Warren said in a brisk voice he sometimes used with tiresome clients. "Sometimes you do go on about trifles."

"Trifles?" She blinked at him with glass eyes. "Yes, I suppose you men would see it as a trifle."

Rachel tried to sound light as she said, "They're the fashion now, you know."

"I was reading just the other day about how young people are becoming so open these days," Mrs. Phillips said in a too-loud voice.

Amelia glanced at her. "Is it the fashion for young men to hide behind beards?" Her voice was sharp.

"Jack's not trying to hide anything, Aunt Amelia." Rachel's laugh sounded like a screech.

Her aunt's vacant eyes pounced. "Do you like it, Rachel, dear?"

She stiffened. "Very much, as a matter of fact. Don't you, Mrs. Phillips?" She glanced at the elegant woman who was to be her mother-in-law.

"Like what?" the woman asked.

"Jack's beard," she answered. "It makes him look distinguished, don't you think?"

"Why, yes, I suppose so." The woman looked puzzled.

Amelia turned her eyes on Mrs. Phillips. "When my Donny suddenly got a notion to grow a beard, he started hiding things from me."

"Donny?" The woman blinked.

"My son."

"Oh, yes." She glanced at her husband, then at Jack. "Yes."

"When a boy has a notion to cover his face —"

"Oh, nonsense!" Warren scoffed. "I told you it's only a trifle."

"What happened to my Donny was not a trifle!"

The Phillips looked uncomfortably into their empty glasses and Carol immediately signaled to the maid who brought a fresh tray of drinks.

"Well, Pete has nothing to hide," Rachel insisted. "I told you that."

"It was a sudden decision, wasn't it?" Amelia gazed at him with piercing eyes. "Wasn't it?"

"Well, I suppose so," he admitted. "I mean, I didn't plan to grow one. I just didn't shave one morning and then another morning and then another." He gave a small laugh.

"You see?" She looked at Rachel.

Feeling her temper rise, Rachel lashed out, "Don's beard

wasn't sudden." They all stared at her. "He told me he'd been thinking about it for some time."

"How much time?" her aunt asked.

"It doesn't matter now."

"Since when did he want a beard?" Amelia demanded.

Rachel was quiet for a moment before answering. "Since he was seventeen."

"I think it's about time to call everyone to dinner, don't you, honey?" Warren gave his wife a pointed look. "There'll be dancing later, Amelia. Remember how we used to practice the waltz to Mama's old phonographs when we were kids? You used to do a mean waltz." He laughed.

But Amelia's eyes were still on her niece. "Why didn't you ever tell me?"

Rachel's anger expanded, and she said in a prickly voice, "Just because you don't approve of beards doesn't mean men shouldn't grow them. The whole world isn't here for your approval."

"Your aunt wasn't implying —" Carol began.

"No, she never implies," Rachel said. "She just thinks she can dictate how people should live their lives. Especially those related to her!"

Jack took Amelia's arm as the woman stared at her niece in bewilderment. "That's the dinner bell. Quaint for Essie to ring a bell, isn't it? Won't you let me take you in?" His soft brown eyes were pleading.

She allowed him to lead her by the arm, but her gaze was still on her niece as they proceeded to the dining room. Carol, with her practicality and decorum, had transformed it into a banquet with small round tables for more intimate conversation and a long buffet table against the wall over which Essie and two hired maids presided.

"Now comes the hard part." Warren's voice was buoyant above the chatter. "Who gets to sit at the table with the bride and groom-to-be?"

Carol slipped next to her husband and whispered something in his ear. His expression remained jovial, but his voice was subdued as he turned to his sister. "Why don't you sit with Rachel and Jack?"

The woman blinked. "I don't think they want me."

Rachel took her arm. "Of course we want you, Aunt Amelia. You're my closest relative, aren't you?" She kissed her cheek. Her aunt's smile was genuine.

Warren made a hearty toast with the champagne, but it felt dry and flat against Rachel's tongue. She observed her aunt's eyes still falling on Jack's face now and then, their tight pupils shiny like hard little rain drops. "I'm sorry about what I said." Amelia's voice was soft. "I didn't mean to offend you."

"I wasn't offended," said Jack with his good-natured grin. "I think it's an interesting theory, actually."

"You offended *me*," Rachel snapped.

"Sweet —" Jack glanced at her.

"I'm sorry, dear." Her aunt laid a hand in hers, and Rachel felt the warmth and softness she remembered as a child.

"Aunt Amelia, you shouldn't have fretted over Don's beard," she said. "All the poets have them."

"Donny was going to be a lawyer," Amelia said.

"He was a poet. A very talented one too."

Her aunt stared at her. "Did he show you his poems?"

"Some of them," she said. "Once, he went down to the Circle Cafe and read a few to the crowd."

In a flimsy voice, her aunt said, "He never showed me any of them."

"Well, you know how artists can be shy about their work," Jack lamented. "I had a college buddy who used to draw and hide his sketch pad under the mattress. Of course, he was drawing nudes." He gave Rachel a lopsided grin that matched his father's. She swatted at him with her napkin, grateful for his attempt to lighten the mood.

"He was never shy with me about anything," Amelia said softly. "We knew everything about one another."

"Maybe that was the trouble," Rachel murmured.

"You and your mother are very close," her aunt pointed out. "Don't you know everything about one another?"

"Not everything." Rachel glanced at Jack.

Well, you have your father to run interference." Amelia looked down at the empty place in front of her.

Jack half rose. "Let me get you some food, Aunt Amelia."

"Would you, sweet?" Rachel gave him a meaningful look.

When he was gone, she turned to her aunt. "I don't want to upset you, but I think if you knew something about Don, it might ease your mind."

"There isn't anything I don't know about Donny." Her aunt said. "Except where he is right now."

"I don't know where he is," said Rachel. "But I can promise you that he's out doing what he wants to do."

Her aunt's eyes shone like globes.

"He didn't flunk out of law school because he wasn't smart enough," she continued. "He flunked out because he wanted to."

Amelia's head seemed to bob over her shoulders. "What on earth are you talking about?"

"He came to me the night he went away," said Rachel. "He told me everything. I know you and Dad thought he couldn't make the grade with his studies. That's not true. He was a good student, very good, in fact."

"He showed me his grades, and they were all bad!"

"And they were," said Rachel. "He chose to make them that way. He could have gotten all A's and B's if he'd wanted to. He didn't want to."

"But why, for heaven's sake?"

"Isn't it obvious, Aunt Amelia?" Rachel sighed. "You pushed it on him, like you pushed so many things on him. He wanted to be a poet, not a lawyer."

"Then why didn't he come to me and say so?"

Rachel glared at her. "You always called his poetry 'silly nonsense.'"

"Well, if I'd known how serious he was about it —"

"You did know he was serious!"

"Perhaps I did." Her aunt's voice shook. "I didn't want him to struggle in life. Your father was more than willing to take him into the firm when he finished college."

"You ought to have given Don a chance," said Rachel. "But you wouldn't, so he had to take it."

Jack came back and put a plate piled with lasagna, Swedish meatballs, herbed asparagus, scalloped potatoes, and salad in front of her. But Amelia left it all untouched, her shoulders hunched as her bright eyes peered at her niece.

"Don told me that night he was going with some of his poet friends," said Rachel.

Her aunt grabbed her forearm with small, clawing fingers. "Where?"

"He wouldn't tell me," Rachel said. "Maybe he didn't know himself."

"How did they go?" Amelia asked.

"Hitched, of course," said Rachel. "Jack and I have done it many times."

"That's so dangerous!" Her aunt covered her mouth with her hand.

"I'm sure no harm came to him if he was with his friends." Jack said in a reassuring voice.

"He's always wanted to travel." Rachel smiled a little. "Did you know that, Aunt Amelia?"

"Of course I knew that." Her aunt picked up the fork and knife but still didn't eat.

"He didn't think he would ever amount to anything as a poet unless he had experiences," said Rachel. "He had to set out on the road, you see."

"The Jack Kerouac approach to writing." Jack chuckled.

"Nonsense!" Amelia said. "He could have stayed right here and written his poetry. I would have helped him."

"That's just it," said Rachel. "There are things we have to do for ourselves. Don't you see that, Aunt Amelia?"

Her aunt looked at her with sorrowful eyes. "I wish I'd known."

"I'm telling you now so you realize Don didn't abandon you." Rachel covered her aunt's hand with hers. "He wanted to be a poet, and he was afraid you would try and stop him."

"I suppose he confided in you about a lot of things." Amelia peered at her.

Rachel speared a Brussel sprout from the plate Pete had brought her. "Cousins always confide in each other."

"You and Donny were close. I know that." She turned to Jack. "His father died in France during the war, you know."

"Yes, I know," Jack said.

"Donny was only two years old. Such a difficult thing, explaining to a child his papa is dead, and it's only him and Mama from now on," she mused.

"He was very lonely," Rachel said. "You didn't know that, did you?"

"Oh, yes, I knew." Her aunt glanced at her. "That I knew."

"I remember how Mom and Dad were always inviting you to dinners and parties," said Rachel. "But you never came. Why?"

"I didn't want to impose," she said.

"But they wanted you to know their friends."

"They were all well above my head," said Amelia. "I didn't want to look like a fool."

Rachel felt her agitation rise. "Maybe Don wouldn't have been so lonely if you had thought a little more about him and a little less about yourself!"

"Rachel." Jack's voice had lost its chipper tone.

Amelia picked at the asparagus in silence. Then, she dropped the fork, and her eyes appealed to Jack again. "Donny used to tell me I was his best friend. I thought that was enough. If I had known he would run away —"

"He didn't run away!" Rachel insisted. "Haven't I just explained it to you?"

Her aunt gave her a helpless look. "You don't understand. To a mother who has nothing else, any moment her child isn't with her is like he's run away."

"He had his own life to live." Rachel felt her throat tighten. "Why can't you understand that?"

"Maybe we should talk about something else," Jack suggested.

Rachel's simmering temper rose to its boiling point. She pushed back her chair. "You just can't face the fact that you've been selfish all these years, Aunt Amelia."

"Selfish?" her aunt echoed without looking at her.

"Your selfishness kept Don in a crucible," said Rachel. "Your selfishness makes you a martyr now." She felt as if she were going to choke. "Do you think you're the only one who suffered when Don left?"

Amelia gave her a tender look. "Oh, I know, dear. I know you've suffered too."

"Don and I were like siblings. And now —" The tears rolled down her cheeks, "— and now, he won't be at my wedding!"

"I'm sure he will." Her aunt's face crumbled with distress. "I'm sure he knows. I'm sure he'll —"

"He won't and you know he won't!" She held her napkin to her face as she felt the eyes looking at her, some with pity, some with curiosity. "Oh, I'm sorry. I'm sorry!" She rushed out of the room.

~~~~~

By the time the coffee was served and one of Rachel's best friends put a Chubby Checker record on the photograph and started to dance the twist, Rachel was almost her bubbly, cheerful self and the incident at the dinner table was all but
~~~~~

forgotten. She danced with Jack and had a few dances with some of the other young men. Then, her father persuaded her to let him put on "Chattanooga Choo Choo" and teach her how to swing dance. The younger people laughed and clapped and a few even tried their hand at it, stumbling all over their partners' feet and filling the high-ceiling space with their silly giggling.

As Rachel took a breather with a glass of water, fanning herself with her handkerchief, she noticed her aunt was not in the room. She slipped her hand out of Jack's and rose. "I think I should apologize to Aunt Amelia, don't you?"

"It would be a nice thing to do," he ventured.

"I shouldn't have gotten so upset." Rachel sighed. "It's not her fault, after all."

"It's not easy to lose a son," her mother murmured.

Rachel stiffened. "She didn't lose a son. He just grew up"

Jack kissed her hand. "Of course, you're right, Rachel. But she doesn't see it that way."

She found her aunt in the bedroom sitting on the purple and blue-trimmed cover on the four-poster bed with the sheath curtains pulled back, the bed that had always made Rachel feel like a queen. An old Scrabble board sat in her lap.

"Aunt Amelia, where did you find it?" Rachel was genuinely delighted. "I thought we'd lost it."

"It was pushed way under the bed," said her aunt.

Rachel blinked, then laughed. "I remember now. Dad threatened to throw it out with all the other old stuff, so I hid it."

"You were always good with words," said Amelia. "I don't think Donny would have come to love words so much if it hadn't been for those weekends here with you."

Rachel felt a wave of relief as she realized her aunt was in one of her subdued moods. She put her arm around her shoulders. "I'm sorry I got upset at dinner."

Her aunt's eyes fell on the game in her lap. "Donny told me

once his happiest days were spent sitting in your living room in front of the fire playing this game."

"He used to call me Princess Scrabble, and I called him The Scrabble Knight." Rachel chuckled at the memory of the two of them with their golden heads bent over the wooden pieces and trays, so intent on winning their war of words.

"Why?"

"Oh, he was always gallant, leaving the letters he knew I would need to win the game. And I, being the princess, always had to win."

"He never told me that either," Amelia murmured. "So many things he never told me."

"Would it have mattered if he did?" Rachel looked at her.

Her aunt's eyes wandered to the pink teddy bear sitting on the bureau. "No, I suppose it wouldn't."

Rachel closed the lace curtains, shielding them from the light from the street. Her eyes and throat burned. "I wish he would at least send me a postcard."

"I expect he doesn't want it to get back to me," said her aunt. "Things have a way of spilling over from one family member to another."

"Maybe he doesn't intend to stay away much longer," Rachel ventured.

"After two years?" Amelia's tone was dismayed. "He'll stay away, perhaps forever. Donny was always headstrong about anything he really wanted."

"You're headstrong too," Rachel mused. "Dad says I take after you."

A shadow appeared around her crow's feet eyes. "That was my undoing, Rachel. Don't let it be yours."

"What do you mean by 'undoing'?"

Her aunt set the game down near the bed with care, as if afraid to upset the pieces inside. "You must believe me when I tell you I thought I was doing the right thing."

Rachel nodded. "It was wrong of me to say you were selfish."

"I don't deny I was selfish," said Amelia. "I didn't see it that way at the time." She turned to her niece. "You see, dear, I was always led to believe you took care of a child so he would take care of you when you got old."

"That's a pretty unfair burden to put on a child, don't you think?"

"Your grandfather didn't think so."

"Grandfather?" Rachel saw the faded photo on her father's desk of the man dressed in a striped, baggy suit with a straw hat who looked very much like him, a man who had died before she was born.

"We were very close," Amelia murmured. "I always believed everything he told me. It never occurred to me he could be wrong."

Rachel took her hand. "No one has to be right or wrong."

"I *was* keeping Donny in a crucible." Her aunt sighed. "A child can only stay locked up for so long before he starts to look for the key."

"All children look for the key when they grow up," Rachel insisted.

Her aunt gave a wry smile. "You were perfectly willing to blame me earlier, and now you're making excuses for me."

"I wasn't blaming," Rachel said. "I was trying to make you see things from Don's point of view."

"I wanted so much for him." Amelia's globe eyes turned almost a pale peach under the lights above the bed. "But it isn't about what the parent wants. It's about what the child wants when he grows up, isn't it?"

Rachel rose. "Let's go back to the party. Dad said he wants to dance a waltz with you, remember?"

But her aunt remained sitting on the bed. "You don't hate me anymore?"

Rachel's eyes filled with tears. "I never hated you, Aunt Amelia. And neither does Don."

"I know Warren always said I was too overprotective," Amelia said. "In his way of thinking, a parent doesn't hover over a child. Your mother and father don't hover. Maybe because they have each other."

"You might have married again," Rachel mused.

"Don't think I didn't have my opportunities!" Her aunt leaned her head back, a little of her old twinkle back in her eyes. "But a husband isn't always the answer, Rachel. I never liked being told what to do."

"Because you're headstrong." Rachel smiled.

Her aunt grabbed both her hands. "That might be your downfall, dear. Or your salvation."

"Aunt Amelia, you're not making any sense."

"I know you were hurt when I said your young man was hiding something under that beard," she said. "Hiding doesn't have to be all about secrets."

Rachel slipped her hands out of her aunt's and rose. "They'll be looking for us."

"When things fall into the status quo, they're like open secrets," her aunt continued. "Like when my father told me Donny would take care of me in my old age. After Tim didn't come back from the war, others told me the same thing. No one was willing to tell me that wasn't what having a child was about."

"What open secret do you think Pete is hiding from me?" Rachel asked.

Amelia peered at her. "I don't know — he seems rather — conventional."

"Is that all?" Rachel felt relieved. "I thought you were going to tell me he's some kind of monster."

"Oh, no! He's a nice young man, very accomplished, very easy-going. Maybe a little too easy-going."

Rachel looked at the wave of lace curtain hanging over the

window. How often she had thought the same thing and even wanted to shake Pete to rattle the grin off his face just so she could see he really was aware of the gray areas of life. It was ironic that, as a lawyer, he was taught to search for the gray areas and yet, in life, he avoided them.

"I want to ask of you one thing," her aunt said. "I know I've no right."

"You're my godmother," said Rachel. "You can ask of me anything you wish."

Amelia rose, looking more dignified than she had in a long time. She looked like a female Napoleon in her dress cut so finely around her shoulders, making the most of her small stature. "If you find yourself wanting to cling to something as if it were the only breath of life — even if it's your own child — remember me. When you start to lose yourself, think of me."

Rachel's eyes filled with tears as she put her arms around her shoulders. "Oh, Aunt Amelia! I don't think I've ever seen you. I mean really *seen* you."

Her aunt said nothing, only squeezed her back with her small hands.

~~~~~

It was one o'clock in the morning when the last guests finally left, waltzing down the walkway in an effort to tease Warren about his "old fogey" dancing. The house was strangely quiet as Carol locked the door. Echoes of the party music and dancing feet still treaded around the living room even though the ensemble had left a long time ago and the phonograph lid was locked. Essie and the hired maids began clearing away the empty coffee cups and small plates still smeared with dessert cream.

Warren put his arm around his daughter. "Everyone had a great time, honey."

"I've never seen my dad swing." Jack grinned. "I didn't think he had it in him."
~~~~~

"He said he was quite a hot potato on the dance floor in his day." said Warren.

Carol took hold of her daughter's arm as they went upstairs. "I saw you patched things up with Aunt Amelia. She seemed happy when she left."

"She was calm," Rachel agreed.

"I'm sorry she made such a scene at dinner." Warren kissed his daughter's forehead. "She's got to get over Don, whether he comes home or not. She's got to get over it, and I told her so."

"You shouldn't have, Dad." Rachel's voice was unusually plucky.

"Why not?" asked her father. "It's the truth. I told her I would call Dr. Marley tomorrow and make an appointment for her."

"Isn't he that psychiatrist you sometimes use as an expert witness?" Jack asked.

"One of the best," said Warren. "He'll set her right."

"He won't make her go to one of those awful places, will he?" Carol hugged her arms around her.

"He'll set her right," was all her husband said.

Rachel lingered in the hallway. "You think that's what she needs? A doctor to 'set her right'?"

"She does tend to blow everything sky high," Carol admitted. "Doctors know about these things, dear." Her voice scattered into an easy smile as she glanced at Jack, who was staying the weekend. "We shouldn't speak of such unpleasant things. Not tonight."

"Might make Jack think twice about marrying into our family," Warren joked.

"I'll tell you about my second cousin Geoffrey sometime," Jack said with a laugh. "He was quite a looney too."

"Stop it!" Rachel fingers clawed at the door. "Stop talking about crazy people. Just because someone has different ways of doing things doesn't make them a looney."

"Now, don't get yourself upset." Jack hugged her shoulders. "We were only teasing."

"It's time you stopped teasing," she snapped. "Always teasing, never taking anything seriously. Why shouldn't Aunt Amelia be upset over Don? He's her son, and he hasn't sent her word in two years!"

Jack looked at Warren. "Do you have any idea where he might be?"

"He's probably in some big city rooming with a few of those Beat poets," said Warren.

"He's somewhere where he doesn't want to be found," Carol put in.

"He's a grown man." Warren's voice was firm. "Twenty years old now. He can do what he likes, whether we approve or not, and he doesn't have to tell us about it, either. That's what I want Amelia to understand."

"How can she understand when everyone's been trying to force her to believe the opposite since he was a child?" Rachel snapped.

Her father eyed her. "You must have had quite a chat with your aunt this evening."

"I did." Rachel's stubborn lip set. "It's too bad you weren't a fly on the wall in my room, Dad. Even you might have understood her differently if you had been."

"Now, honey." Her father patted her arm. "We're all tired."

Carol, as usual, took the cue to begin her domestic arrangements, and she motioned toward Jack, explaining about the room she had set for him, the plans they had tomorrow to go to Chinatown, which he hadn't seen since he was a boy. Rachel followed them, listening with only half her attention, as the other half was still on what her father said about her aunt.

She imagined how many men in suits and eyeglasses Amelia had encountered as a young mother who smiled and condescended over her, their eyes gazing with pity on the poor war widow with a toddler son to raise on her own and, surely, no experience in the world and not much brains, not with that flightiness of hers. She certainly needed their advice. And she got it — so much of it that she hadn't a clue now, twenty years later, who she was.

"Let's go out to the porch," she said to Jack when her mother left them alone. "There's such a nice breeze. I feel like some air."

She led him downstairs to the front of the house where the moths already showed their enthusiasm for the milky lights sprinkling the ceiling. They flitted around undisturbed as she and Jack settled on the porch glider.

"What *did* you and your aunt talk about?" he ventured.

"So many things," she said. "Things you wouldn't be interested in.

"Girl talk," he said with a smile. "I get it."

"In a way it was girl talk," she murmured. "Aunt Amelia wanted to explain."

"What was there to explain?"

"Oh, why she was always so over-involved with Don's life," said Rachel. "I'm sure this Dr. — what's his name?"

"Dr. Marley."

"I'm sure Dr Marley will have some fancy clinical name for it."

"You're worried about that, aren't you?" He took her hand. "I've met him a few times, Rachel. He's a very decent fellow."

"He'll probably say she's neurotic," Rachel said. "And whatever other scientific-sounding nonsense he can think of."

"He's a professional psychiatrist," Jack argued. "If they use those words, they do it for a reason."

"I wonder if it ever occurred to anyone that she didn't have much of a choice." Rachel leaned her head back on the cushion as Jack's long legs swung the couch gently back and forth. "She was alone with a child to raise. People were expecting things of her. Others made promises."

"What sort of promises?"

"As a man, I don't think you would understand."

"That's girl talk for you," he said with a grin. "Nobody can understand but the girls."

She glared at him. "Jack, why do you always have to make a joke out of everything?"

He blinked at her. "You said once you liked how I took everything so lightly."

"Not everything," she murmured. "Some things are serious."

He was annoyed now. "You're not going to start treating me like your aunt treated her son, are you?"

"What do you mean?" Her fists clenched against the cushion.

"Wanting me to be something I'm not."

She leaned over and kissed him. "I'm marrying you for who you are, not for who I expect you to be."

"We all have our expectations," Jack mused. "My dad expected me to become a partner in his firm pretty much since the day I was born. I never considered disappointing him by making other plans."

"I thought you liked the law."

"I do," he said. "Some parts of it. Others, I could do without. But it's like that with everything, isn't it?"

She gave him a sharp look. "And me? What do you expect of me?"

He was genuinely surprised by the question. She could see how his eyes were intent on the plant sitting on the porch that flopped its heart-shaped leaves against the wind. Two of them were dry and yellow. "Why, I don't know."

"I think you do," she said quietly.

"I guess I haven't thought much about it." His joking tone was gone. "We never discussed what we expect of one another after we're married."

"Isn't it time we did?"

"Why?" he challenged. "We're marrying each other because we're in love, not because we expect certain things from one another. Isn't that right?"

She laughed and snuggled against his strong shoulder. "And they say women are the sentimentalists!"

"Well, I don't see we have to expect anything from one another," he said. "Except to love, honor, and obey."

The last word plucked at her nerves like hard fingers on taunt strings. She sat up. "That's it, isn't it? That's what you expect. Love, honor, and *obey.*"

"I forgot for a minute how much most brides balk at that word nowadays," he said. "Don't worry, sweet. We'll replace it with something else."

"Something else," she murmured. "With what? Love, honor, and devote?"

"Well, naturally, we'll be devoted to one another and to our kids," he said.

"But you'll be devoted to your work too."

"Oh, don't you worry." He kissed her on the nose. "I won't be one of those lawyers who comes home at midnight and goes out again at five, working seven days a week. I'll spend plenty of time with you and the kids."

"You like kids, don't you, Jack?"

"Love 'em!" He smiled. "You'll laugh and call me sentimental if I tell you something."

"I won't." Her voice softened. "Tell me."

"You know how some girls talk about having five or eight or ten kids when they grow up? That's the sort of thing I've always wanted too. I guess being an only child makes me want lots of kids in the house."

"You want us to have eight or ten children?" She looked into the empty space of black in the street hidden by night.

"Oh, we don't have to have that many," he said. "Five or six will do."

"And me?" she asked. "What do I do?" She was peering at him now, seeing his illuminated face under the lights. "I mean it, Jack.

What do I do when you'll have your work along with your family?"

"Why, take care of the kids, of course," he said with a sigh. "Rachel, I'm too tired for guessing games right now."

"You want me to love, honor, and devote," she said. "To you and the kids. Do I have that right?"

"Well, naturally," he said. "Just as I'll be devoted to you and our kids."

"And to what else?" She rose and paced the porch. "Your work, your club, your lawyer colleagues, your football team, oh, millions of other things. You'll be devoted to yourself too."

He chuckled. "You always seem to choose the strangest times for philosophical discussions."

"I'm not being philosophical," she insisted. "I'm actually being very, very practical." She bent forward so she could meet his eyes. "I'm beginning to think Aunt Amelia was right. You were hiding something under that beard."

"Rachel, have I ever told you that you can be tiresome sometimes?" He leaned his head back and closed his eyes.

"You had these ideas about how things will be when we're married, but you wouldn't have told me if I hadn't asked," she said. "You always talk about how your mother's had her own life separate from your father's."

"But not separate from me," he said. "I mean, so much of what Mom did involved things like my hobbies and activities. Isn't that what every mother does?"

The genuine confusion on his face struck Rachel as amusing, and she threw her head back and laughed. Her laugher echoed into the night, almost making the street lights waver.

"I don't see anything funny in it," Jack snapped.

"Your mother is more like Aunt Amelia than you realize," she said. "Maybe that's what people expect from women, really expect from them."

"Rachel." His voice took on the tone that she had heard when he practiced arguing a case in front of her. "What is it you're trying to say?"

"I'm asking a question," she said. "You want me to be like your mother. What if I can't be?"

"You mean, you don't want kids?" For the first time since Rachel had met him, his face looked pale with fear.

"Of course I want kids," she reassured him. "I want to devote my time to you and our kids. But I also want to devote some time to myself."

"Well, I never implied you shouldn't," he said. "I told you how my mom always had her committees and clubs."

"I don't mean that," she said. "I mean, something that is truly *me* and not an extension of other people."

"You mean a career?" He stiffened. "I know that's supposed to be fashionable these days."

"Well, if you can have a beard if it's fashionable, why can't I have a career?" She retorted.

"They're not the same thing, and you know it!"

"I didn't say I wanted one," she said in a low voice. "I don't know what I want. That's what I'm trying to tell you. And I don't want to bury that because I have a good life handed to me on a silver platter."

"Oh, I guess you could get yourself a little job, if you really want to work," he said. "After the kids start going to school, of course."

She sank back onto the couch swing, perched at the other end. "That wasn't what I meant either, Jack."

"I told you I was too tired for guessing games." He yawned.

"I'll make it plain, then." She faced him. "I don't want to end up like Aunt Amelia."

"That's something you'll never have to worry about, sweet." He petted her arm. "I think your dad's probably right. Your aunt, well, she's had this tragedy in her life and it's affected her mind. Dr. Marley will settle her."

"No," Rachel said. "No doctor can do that. She needed to settle herself a long time ago instead of letting others settle things for her."

"Who settled things for her?"

Rachel shivered and wrapped her arms around herself, feeling the breeze through her dress. "You wouldn't understand."

"Well, it's too late now," Jack rose and stretched. "Now she needs a doctor."

"Yes, it's too late," said Rachel. "For Aunt Amelia, maybe. But it isn't too late for me."

He stood gaping. "What do you mean?"

"Oh, nothing."

"For a minute there, it sounded like you were breaking off our engagement."

She put her arms around his neck. "I want to marry you, just as we planned. But we have to talk more about what we expect of one another before we do."

"Whatever you say, sweet." He kissed her neck. "As long as it's not tonight."

"No," she said. "We'll both think clearer in the morning."

She entered her bedroom, the light still burning from her aunt's earlier visit. The clingy cover was a little bent, and the Scrabble game lay on the floor where Amelia had left it. Rachel opened the box and fingered the skewed wooden letters. She started sifting through them and came up with the letters she wanted. She spelled out WIFE, BOY, GIRL, AND. What came after the AND? Because of Amelia, it would never be too late to find out.

TWO SIDES OF LIFE

The morning of her forty-second birthday, Leanne felt a strange frost in the air. It was October, and the California sun usually gleamed in Palo Alto during that time of year so there was nothing to account for the morning chill. She had been rising earlier since Linda left for Purdue, even earlier than Calvin when he was scheduled to teach an eight o'clock lab.

Their gingerbread house on the lot owned by the university was compact so even when she was in the kitchen, she could hear Calvin snore above the bacon spitting in the pan. No matter how soundly he slept, he always seemed to know when breakfast was ready. He would appear in a stiff-collared shirt, tailored slacks that fit just below his belly, and no tie. The head of the chemical engineering department hinted more than once this was not considered "dressy" enough for a university professor, but Calvin, as usual, assumed he was right and the head was wrong and continued with his habits. His narrow glasses made his eyes look buggy that morning, and his balding head shone splotchy in the morning light.

He eased his chair away from the table to make room for his girth and mumbled a "happy birthday" as he did so. Leanne acknowledged him with a quick nod as she slid the scrambled eggs onto the plate and placed them in front of him.

"I have Peters and Godwin to see after classes today," he said. "Their projects are due in a few weeks. But I've reserved a table at Jathe's for six tonight."

"Good of you," she murmured as she sat down to coffee and toast.

"What are your plans today?" He poured a generous amount of ketchup on the side of his plate and began to eat his eggs noisily. Leanne tried not to wince.

"Amber said she might stop by."

"To give you some birthday mantra, no doubt." His tone was half-joking and half-sneering.

"She might," she answered in a curt voice.

"I thought you could go to the Jarvises' today, around noon."

"Why would I want to do that?" she asked. "He's your assistant, not mine."

"Don't be so quick on the trigger, honey," he said.

She gritted her teeth at the way he always spoke in clichés. "Why do you want me to go to the Jarvises'?"

"I didn't say I *wanted* you to go. Paul told me Arnold is having a birthday party today, and the boy invited his entire class."

"Children usually do at that age," Leanne said.

"There should be lots of kids there," he continued. "Paul's going to be home, of course. But he's a little concerned about Arlene."

"I'm sure if Arlene can wrestle with cancer cells in a petri dish, she can hand out party hats and cake to children." Leanne poured herself another cup of coffee.

"I don't think Paul's worried about that."

"Well, then?"

He plucked another slice of bread from the toaster between his thick fingers. "I just thought if you went over there and offered to help, it might be a nice gesture."

Leanne's cup came down into the saucer. "Are you finding things for me to do now, Cal?"

"Well, Linda's only been gone a few months, and I thought you might take more of an interest in our neighbors," he hedged.

"Because without the children, my day must be empty," she finished, glaring at him. "Yes, you would think that, wouldn't you?"

"And just what *do* you do all day?" His shoulders squared for an argument.

"I keep busy." She rose and took away the empty plates.

"With those cuckoo charts of yours?" His moist eyes peered at her.

She turned away from him and began to take deep breaths through her nose and exhaling out her mouth, just as Amber, her astrology teacher and a psychologist, had taught her. In the two months since Linda had been gone, she had come to realize how tightly she had held in her breath, always on her guard that what she said and did wouldn't end up in an argument with Calvin. In twenty-two years of marriage, she learned not to fight with him when his mind picked up a combative spark just as dry wood picked up a flame. For Calvin, being right was more important than anything else in the world, and he was a formidable opponent in word battles. When she told Amber, the woman had looked at her with pity in her dark eyes and remarked, "He's afraid you'll say something about him that he doesn't want to hear." Leanne learned to stop the argument before it started because it would always end with her feeling bruised and battered by his inexhaustible reasoning.

"I appreciate the thought, but I don't need you to find preoccupations for me," she said carefully.

"This isn't a preoccupation," he answered. "It's only one afternoon. And you would be helping me out."

"How would my being at the birthday party help you out?"

She scrubbed the plate Calvin had just used as if it had been stored in the attic for twenty years.

"Paul is the best assistant I've ever had," he said. "We're thinking of offering him a faculty position next year. Part-time, of course, so it won't pay much. But if you make his wife happy, you make him happy."

"And that will make you happy?" she threw out.

He rose. "You used to be a nice person, always ready to help anyone who needed it and without anybody asking."

"Maybe I've learned to take some time for myself, now that I'm over forty."

"Just because you're over forty doesn't mean you have to be selfish!" He dumped the empty toast plate in the sink, letting the crumbs scatter around the drain in the way she hated.

Leanne took another deep breath. Calvin could be like a clock that had just been rewound, ready to go on with the battle by meeting everything she said with a counterattack. She could already feel her head buzzing and her eyes half-drooping from the tiresomeness. "I finished with children's parties years ago, Cal."

"Well, another one won't hurt, will it?" He patted her shoulder. "You don't have to do much. Just stand there and supervise."

"Amber is supposed to stop by —"

"Maybe she'll get one of her callings from the stars, or whatever it is, and she won't show up," he said. "She didn't actually promise to come by, did she?"

"No, that's true," Leanne admitted.

"It would be a nice thing," he mumbled as he straightened the collar of his shirt under the folds of flesh on his chin.

"You keep saying that!"

"Will you go?"

She sighed. "I might look in. Noon, you said?"

He picked up his briefcase with one of his toothy grins. "I'll be home by five in time to dress for Jathe's."

Amber called Leanne around eleven and said she wouldn't be able to stop by after all, as she would be doing some readings at a local woman's community center. She invited Leanne to come along, but Leanne, remembering Calvin's buzzing voice, said, "I'll be attending a birthday party."

Paul answered the door and looked gratified when she extended her offer to help. "I hope I didn't put you out," he said. "I only mentioned it to Calvin in passing."

"Calvin often looks like he isn't listening when he is." She gave him her coat to hang. "I don't want to impose."

"You could never do that, Leanne," he said with a smile.

Although Paul had been Calvin's assistant for three years, Leanne had never been to his home. The first thing she noticed when she walked into their bungalow was how different it was from others the university reserved for doctoral students. It had modern furnishings, complete with a shaggy rug and box cushion chairs in the living room and shades of earthy green, brown, and red.

As she trailed after him, she murmured, "This isn't quite what I expected."

Paul opened the glass door to the backyard where Leanne could see small tables full of children sitting with party hats and paper horns. "What do you mean?"

"I remember you telling me at that faculty party about your collection of Impressionist sculptures." She felt her face redden. "I thought you would have them on display. You ought to!"

"Arlene's grandfather left her some money." Paul said. "We used it to modernize the house, as she didn't want to live in an atmosphere of antiquity."

"What a pity," she murmured as she saw Paul's wife approaching them.

Arlene, a doctoral biology student, was a mousy woman who looked much younger than her twenty-six years. Leanne often thought she inserted herself into the conversations held by the science and engineering professors at university functions a little too boldly, as if she were too good to associate with the professors' wives. Leanne found herself tongue-tied under the scrutiny of Arlene's orb-shaped eyes bearing into her like an eagle trying to decide whether the dead carcass in front of her was worth the feast.

"Nice of you to come." Her voice deep and slow. "Calvin told Paul you probably would."

"I'm sure he did." Leanne tried to control her annoyance at her husband's pompous presumption.

"I told Paul it really wasn't necessary to mention it to him. We have everything under control."

"It's no trouble." Over Arlene's shoulder, she saw one little boy jump from his chair and begin chasing a little girl around the table.

"Paul, honey, go and calm them down, won't you?" Arlene sighed. "Kids must have their fun, mustn't they?" The metallic smile on her pale lips confirmed Leanne's suspicion: Arlene Jarvis was one of those glossy women who was always trying to prove to everyone, but mostly to herself, that she could be as good a mother as she was a scientist.

As Leanne helped serve the pigs in a blanket and potato chips to the children, she couldn't help but feel Arlene's idea of motherhood was as mechanical as the biological experiments she conducted. The young woman kept picking at her son's shirt and petting down the jumping curls on his head. Her deep voice became sticky when Paul produced a spaniel puppy in a box with a bow around its neck, and when Arnold, jumped up to snatch it out of his father's hands, she insisted he return to the table because "you have guests, Arnie."

The afternoon wore on, and as Arnold opened the rest of his presents, delivering an overly polite "thank you" to each child in turn, Leanne resented the control Arlene seemed to possess. Her mind traced back to her own mother, a small woman whose beauty drew people to her like a powerful light. Her mother had been ambitious and aggressive too, though her domain was more domestic. She would begin complaining of their tiny house the moment Leanne's father came home dragging his robust frame, his eyes nearly wincing from having bent over his accounting books all day. For years, her mother was determined they should build her dream house. She squandered any money she could lay her hands on, forcing Leanne and her brothers to go without eggs for breakfast or meat in the stew for dinner, and wouldn't buy them new pencils for school but made them wear down their old ones to the nib. Her mother cared more about lace curtains than about her children's pencils.

Leanne's eyes fell on Paul. A few dark curls fell across his forehead, and his eyes were bright as he stood against the patio door, his long arms folded behind him. He kept looking at his son, trying to send a reassuring message that would relieve him of his mother's overbearing presence. He suddenly turned his head and caught Leanne's gaze. She saw in them the helpless look of a lost boy.

She approached Arlene and, in a soft voice, suggested, "Maybe the children could play some sort of game now that the presents are all opened. It would do them good to get up and move around a bit. And Paul and I could clear away the paper and bows for you."

"I can't think why Paul insisted on being here." Arlene's voice cracked a little as she brushed a wet napkin against a stain of ketchup on her tailored suit. "He had a date to play golf with some of his colleagues."

"He wanted to be here for his son's birthday, naturally." Leanne knew she sounded condescending, and she knew Arlene felt it.

The young woman's eyes narrowed, though she didn't look up from her task of cleaning the stain. "You would think I can't give my son a pleasant party, the way there are so many people hovering around." Suddenly, her head snapped up, and she glared at Leanne. "That's why he and Calvin arranged for you to come, isn't it?"

Leanne stiffened. "No one arranged for me to come, Arlene. Calvin did mention it to me this morning, but I came on my own." She retreated to the tree where the spaniel puppy was now asleep.

A few moments later, the children were on the lawn playing Blind Man's Bluff, laughing and running around. Arlene, however, rejected with a stoic determination Paul's offer to help with the mess, nodding toward Leanne as she spoke in a low tone.

Paul joined her in a few moments later. "Arlene tries so hard with everything she does," he said. "But she always has to have everything go right."

"Calvin is a perfectionist too." Leanne nodded.

"They're so proud of her in the department," he continued as they watched Arlene fold a piece of wrapping paper neatly in the pile of folded paper near the patio door to be taken inside. "She's on her way to discovering some kind of formula to help doctors detect breast cancer."

"That's admirable," she said.

"They asked her to work today, but she told them she couldn't because of the birthday party," he continued.

"I could have come earlier, and we could have handled the party ourselves," Leanne said. "There was no need for your wife to give up her precious lab time." She couldn't help but think how Arlene probably cared more about her experiments than her own son, just as her mother had cared more about her lace curtains.

He glanced at her, his eyes like gray beads. "You judge her harshly, don't you?"

Leanne felt a sting of shame in her eyes. "Do I?"

"Not just you. Your entire generation." He continued to look at the game, which had now grown livelier with Arnold playing the blind man. "I think it's because you all made kids your full-time job."

"Kids *are* a full-time job," Leanne insisted.

"Arlene says women today can have a career and a family if they just balance everything correctly," he said. "It's what she's trying to do, and so are most of the girls who graduated with her." He looked at her again. "Do you think a woman who has a career can't be a good wife and mother too?"

She felt the breeze around her turn into waves, returning the strange chill she felt earlier that morning. The noise of happy children dimmed, replaced by the loud caw of birds. She realized they were standing under a nest where baby birds chirped out their starvation. She saw the head of the mother, its grim beak set, and its gorging eyes searching the ground. She recognized the basic instinct of a mother to protect her children.

"I think any woman can do anything if she sets her mind to it," she said softly. "I can see Arlene has her mind set on it. I've no right to judge her, and I'm sorry I did."

"Oh, I don't blame you," he said. "I do the same thing myself sometimes, like when I've seen her going into the den and locking the door. Arnold looks after her like a lost puppy."

"She has no choice." The veil of hostility that had been weighing over Leanne's eyes lifted with the chattering of the baby birds. "She wants to be more than what women of my generation were."

"I didn't mean to insult you, Leanne, honestly," he said. "I shouldn't judge her either. I'm away all day while she's left with everything on her hands. Just like I'm sure Calvin left you. Though the way he talks, you'd think he was the one who fed, bathed, and diapered your kids." He chuckled.

"In his mind, that's exactly what he did," she said in a brusque voice.

"Oh, fathers have it rough too," he insisted. "We do the best we can, but it's always go, go, go. Doesn't matter if we're young or old, it's all the same."

"It's the same for us wives too," she said softly. "Young and old. Occupation: housewife or occupation: biologist."

The children had now returned to the table, their eyes feasting on the cake Arlene was carrying out. She balanced it precariously in both her hands, visibly nervous that it might topple while the children were singing "Happy Birthday" at the top of their lungs.

"I must get the ice cream," he said. "Arlene has everything timed to the minute." He rushed inside.

Leanne moved closer to the table and joined in the singing, though her voice trailed off in the wake of the cheery little tones. As Arlene lowered her hands to set the cake down in front of Arnold, it began to tilt. She managed to catch it in time, but Leanne saw the gleam of panic in her eyes and the shaking hands that lay the cake down carefully in front of her son. She saw how wrong she was about the young woman caring more for her experiments than for her home. She imagined if it were a culture or a test tube in her hand that had dropped, Arlene would have been annoyed, possibly angry at herself for her carelessness, but her face would never have shown such whitened terror.

She realized she had, in fact, been judging Arlene for months as she watched the pretty, self-possessed young woman in conversations with professors, sparring with their ideas and forcing them to look at her rather than through her. It wasn't so much jealousy that Arlene had the respect of these intellectual men, though that was, maybe, part of it. It was the way Arlene was juggling everything, even if a little shaky at times, that made her feel resentful. No one had ever offered Leanne any option other than marriage and motherhood. They only expected her to be content with that and nothing else.

Through her work with Amber, she had come to see how she felt, at times, the cage bars of that expectation closing in on her.

Now she saw they were the same bars that closed Arlene in as a biologist. She and Paul's wife were two canaries in a cage — one yellow and one white, perhaps, but chirping out the same song, fluttering and waiting to be fed.

When Paul came out with the ice cream, Arlene smiled and handed him the cake knife. "I think you should do the honors, honey."

Leanne watched as Arlene struggled with the ice cream, digging into the box with force. Without a word, she took the scoop from her and began placing ice cream into the small bowls, handing them around the table. Arlene watched with arms folded how Leanne made perfectly round vanilla hoops so that each child received the exact same portion.

"You must have worked in an ice cream parlor before you were married." The grizzled voice came out dripping with sarcasm.

Leanne shook her head and said with a gentle smile, "I've just attended a lot of children's parties."

"I'm not at my best today," the young woman lamented. "I have a lot of important things on my mind. You might say they're even life-changing. The lab wanted me —"

"Yes, Paul told me." Leanne closed the ice cream box and set the scooper down on a napkin so it wouldn't stain the table.

Arlene glared at her husband, who was busy with the cake. "I didn't know he was in the habit of telling the neighborhood housewives my business."

"My husband is his faculty mentor," Leanne reminded her.

"I hope you won't tell *him*," Arlene continued with the icy voice. "Frankly, Leanne, I think your husband is a boor when it comes to women."

Leanne gave her a satisfied look. "So do I."

The young woman gasped as she held the back of her son's chair, clearly taken aback.

Leanne wiped her hands on a clean napkin and continued, "I

saw the party favors on the kitchen table on my way in. Do you think it's a good time to hand them out?"

Arlene stiffened into a perfect slinky statue. "*I'll* decide when it's time."

"I'm sure it will be the right time," said Leanne.

The young woman eyed her. "Don't think I don't know what women like you think of women like me. Well, I can hand out my own party favors, thank you very much!" The last made her voice rise over the chattering of children and they instantly stopped with the fearful sense children had that an argument was taking place.

"I only wanted to help," Leanne said in a low tone.

"Because women like you think women like me need help." The grizzled voice continued, "Well we don't. We're young, and we can do more than your generation ever could."

Leanne blinked at the stormy face, seeing the lines form on Arlene's forehead that made her look ten years older. "You're lucky, then."

Paul, now finished with the cake, took Leanne's arm. "Maybe you'd like to see my collection, Leanne? I remember you mentioned that at the faculty party."

Arlene's face crumbled a little and she looked her real age again. "Yes, let Paul show you his collection. I'm sure you'll like it." She bent over Arnold's shoulder, then glanced at Leanne. "I appreciate your kindness. Really."

Leanne would have liked to stay, but Paul was already leading her inside the house. She followed him down the small hallway and past two rooms until they reached a narrow flight of stairs.

"It's small right now," he said as he turned on the light. "We're going to find a proper way of displaying them when we get the money."

They moved slowly, walking a little sideways to avoid bumping into the walls. "Why not put them in the den or the living room?" she asked, out of breath from climbing the narrow staircase.

"Arlene doesn't think they go with the house. The Victorian era isn't my wife's favorite. She says it was the most oppressive time in history for women."

"Oh, I don't know." She gazed around the room. "I don't think it's very different from what we live today. No, not so very different."

They entered a small space with paneled roofing that showed off a brilliant blue sky. One side of the room had three covered lumps and the other had two.

"I told you the collection isn't very big," Paul mumbled as he slid the sheets off the sculptures.

"It's fine work." Leanne moved closer to the trio. She examined the worn faces and rough hem of petticoats on the women as they did their women's work while children flitted around them.

"That's Hertha Boythorn," he said.

"I don't think I know her."

"She was a contemporary of Mary Cassatt," he said. "Much less well known, of course. She went on to do poster art in the early twentieth century, advertising soap ads and things."

"I can see why," said Leanne.

"When I have the money, I'll have them properly cleaned," Paul continued. "Then you'll really be able to see the children's faces."

"And the faces of the women," Leanne chimed in.

"Yes, of course," he said. "These are my real pride and joy." He uncovered two small marble figures. "Have you seen De Chirico's painting of the Muses?" She shook her head. "Reinhold English — he's the sculptor — got hold of a replica soon after the first world war and modeled these after the figures in the painting. De Chirico was an anti-Impressionist, of course. But I think you'll find these to your liking."

She was struck by the way the afternoon light filtered through the frosty glass, making the gentle waves on the women's hair and robes look as if they were really moving. One figure held a gloomy mask and a saber while the other rested a clownish mask on her knee, a shepherd's crook leaning against her shoulder.

"I'm not familiar with the Muses," she admitted.

"I wouldn't expect you to be." He sat on a box in the corner. It was too low for his long legs, and he looked like a grasshopper resting on a tree stump. "The one with the sword is Melpomene, the Muse of Tragedy. Her sister, Thalia, is the Muse of Comedy."

"I see," Leanne said. "The two sides of life. Sadness and joy."

"I never thought of it that way," he said. "I've always admired how women can get to the heart of something while we men just circle around until we hit on the right words."

She couldn't help but laugh. It was the perfect description of the way she and Calvin communicated. He could make intricate explanations of even the tritest television commercial with his "circling around" while she always reduced the circular arguments and explanations he gave into one thought or idea. It was something he had told her more than once he admired in her.

"I know they're more Art Deco than Impressionism —" Paul was saying.

"I like them." She looked into the women's globe eyes. They were not entirely devoid of expression.

"I'm not sure I do," he admitted.

"Why?"

"They're a little too simplistic for my taste." His gaze wandered to the glass roof. "That's why I like the Impressionists. So many images go into their work."

"Because they 'circle around' the subject?" she asked with a smile.

"Arlene likes these better too," he said. "I think she would even agree to put them in the living room if they weren't so different from the rest of the decor."

"I read it's fashionable nowadays to mix old and new."

"Arlene isn't really interested in what's fashionable," he said. "She's interested in what looks aesthetic and organized."

As they went down the stairs, she asked, "If you don't like the English sculptures, why did you buy them?"

"For posterity." He gave her a knowing look. "They cost a pretty penny — English didn't do many sculptures in his lifetime — but we were able to get them with the money Arlene's grandfather left her."

In a vague tone, she said, "You used your wife's money to buy art?"

"It's an investment, Leanne." His voice grew stubborn, making her realize it was not the first time he had heard this. "She agreed they would be worth a lot of money someday, and we could leave them to our children."

"I thought you said she spent her money on modern furniture."

He smiled as he switched off the light in the stairway. "That was only part of it. The rest went for the sculptures."

Arlene met them as they reached the living room. It was clear the party was finished from the drifting voices of mothers fretting over their children. "What do you think of Paul's women?" She swung her arm through his.

"Leanne thinks they represent the two sides of life," said her husband.

"How clever of you." Arlene sounded sincere. "I don't understand all the symbolism, of course, but I like the way the ladies look."

"You should put them where you can see them," Leanne said as Paul helped her with her coat. "The living room would be an ideal place."

"Don't you think people who visit us might get a little uneasy with those eyes staring at them?" Arlene laughed.

"Let them!" Leanne was surprised by her own fierceness. "Women don't make history unless they make people uneasy."

"I wouldn't have expected that from you, Leanne." Paul looked less than amused.

"Why not?" asked his wife. "Women have been screaming their rage for centuries, even if no one has been listening." She took Leanne's hands in hers. "Thank you for coming over to help. Forgive me if I was ill-tempered."

Leanne smiled. "I enjoyed the party. Sometimes I forget how children can get so excited over little things like ice cream and cake." She paused on the front porch, glancing back at the young couple. "Arlene, if you ever need help — with anything — call me."

The young woman did not answer, but her eyes and lips, which had been tightened throughout the afternoon, eased, reminding Leanne of Thalia's laughing mask.

~~~~~

That evening, she felt as if she and Calvin were entering Jathe's with the awkward stumble of teenagers at a fancy dress ball. The reception area smelled of fresh-cut roses, and the stereo played a sweet Brahms sonata over their heads. She peered into the dining room and saw red tablecloths and gold-rimmed china. Near the door, fish floated in a silent aquarium, their eyes studying the people waiting for their tables.

She took off her gloves. "I'm surprised you decided on Jathe's."

"Why is that?" He was immediately defensives.

"You usually hate fancy places like this."

"But *you* don't," he said. "And it's your birthday, so I didn't see any harm in going hoity-toity for once."

"You did this for me?"

"I didn't do it for me," he said with the crooked grin.

Her voice softened. "That was nice of you, Cal."

But as they stood waiting to be served, her heart beat faster as she glanced once more at the dining area. She hadn't sat alone
~~~~~

with Calvin at a table for years. Even when Bill and Linda were teenagers, she and her husband passed the dinner hour in virtual silence, like two children whose teachers had forced them to sit together during lunch hour.

"You'd think in these hoity-toity places, they'd have quick service," Calvin grumbled, adjusting the tie around his neck.

"Stop using that expression!" Leanne hissed. "It's an insult."

"You're touchy tonight," her husband sulked. "You've been touchy all day. I thought with the party this afternoon, you'd be in a better mood."

"I *was* in a good mood," she said.

"You told me you enjoyed being with the kids."

"I did," she said. "But it's a little jarring, going from balloons and Blind Man's Bluff to this sort of elegant place."

Calvin cleared his throat. "Where did you get your hoity-toity notions anyway? Your pop was a pretty down-to-earth fellow as far as I can remember."

She pretended to concentrate on a spot on her glove. "They're not notions, Cal. It's called quality of life." She stole a glance at him, drumming his fingers on the *Please wait to be seated* sign. He caught her eyes and gave her a quick smile. She felt a wave of pity for him. It wasn't his fault he had grown up with a barbaric father whose stoicism had taken to the belief of "spare the rod, spoil the child".

A young woman with a platinum bob rushed toward them, apologizing. "We're a little short-staffed tonight. I'll get a table cleared for you right away, all right?" She gave them a pert smile.

"Seems like you would have plenty of tables cleared already, young lady," Calvin rumbled. "For the next time, I suggest —"

"She doesn't need your suggestions, Cal," Leanne said in a low voice so the young woman, whose attention was on her seating chart, wouldn't hear.

"I don't see it does any harm to make a suggestion," Calvin insisted.

"It doesn't when someone asks for it," said Leanne.

"People usually welcome good advice even if they don't ask for it."

She had done it — set off the spark on the dry wood that would start the battle of words. She sighed. "You're right, dear."

"I have lots more experience than she does, and it's not as if —"

"I said you're right!" Leanne took a quick, deep breath. "Isn't that enough?"

She heard him mumble, "You wouldn't be like this if Linda were going to Stanford instead of Purdue."

Leanne felt the muscles in her stomach tighten. She had tried to explain to Calvin when Bill left home how the echoing shifts in the house terrified her and made her feel so alone. She had tried to get him interested in her books on astronomy so he could be as comforted by the vastness of the universe as she was. But the moment she unfolded the constellation maps or opened the newspaper to read the horoscope, her husband frowned, saying, "I only hope you're not going turn into one of those cuckoo women who waste their time meditating and speaking to the stars all the time, Leanne." The way he used words like *cuckoo* and *hoity-toity*, like some pre-war curmudgeon grated her nerves. After Linda left for college, she stopped talking to him at all about anything more important than whether the soup was hot enough or the paper would arrive on time.

"You can't force people to learn from your experience all the time, Cal."

"Maybe not," he said. "But you can try to convince them of what's good for them."

She sunk into a chair a woman had vacated in the reception area. "You may feel that way but many of us don't."

He squatted on the bench beside her, his rotund figure taking up half the space. "Kids just need to be spoiled less, that's all."

"I suppose you mean by mothers like me?" She eyed him.

"You've told me often enough how I indulged Bill and Linda too much."

"You acted as if there was no other life more important to you than theirs."

"Maybe I did," she said. "What else was there for me?"

"I wouldn't be surprised if Bill turns out to be some namby-pamby because of you."

"Oh, Cal!"

"Even if he did make a big show of joining the Marines," he grumbled.

"How can you say that when he might be sent to Vietnam any day now?"

"We have no business being there," Calvin scoffed. "Let them settle it among themselves."

"We're already there." Leanne felt her head grow heavy. "Or have you forgotten?"

"Bill isn't there and never will be." he pulled at his tie again. "He'll get out of it somehow."

"No, he won't," Leanne said with a sigh. "That's what worries me."

"You're always worrying," he countered. "In my house, the men never talked about war or politics or business in front of women. We knew where it would get us."

"Well, in *my* house, we did," Leanne snapped. "My mother and I followed the war in Europe and the Pacific more closely than my father did."

"And look where it's gotten you," he countered. "Talking about things you know nothing about."

Leanne turned away, taking deep breaths. In a calmer tone, she said, "And I suppose you think it's wrong of Linda to want to be a commercial pilot?"

"I never heard of anything so silly," he said. "A girl going off to Purdue to study Aeronautics and Astronautics!"

"Amelia Earhart was once on their staff," Leanne challenged, feeling the circular battle play into her head like a spinning wheel.

"Linda will probably end up being a flight attendant anyway," he sniffed. "She never was one for book learning."

"That's an awful thing to say about your own daughter!"

The girl with the Sandra Dee bob appeared with her plastic smile. "I can seat you now. We have a lovely courtyard, in case —"

"We'll sit inside," Calvin said as he heaved himself up.

As the hostess led them through the candlelit room, Leanne began to relax. There were more people there than she first thought. It was only the hushed speech that had given the illusion of emptiness. She glanced at their faces curved with pleasant emotions like humor, joy, and tranquility, feeling as if she were watching a pantomime. She longed to fit in among them, and she was determined that she and Calvin would have a peaceful evening.

Her husband, too, seemed determined they should enjoy themselves, as he backed down from his earlier arguing and rushed forward, pulling back the chair for her. He even bowed a little as she scooted forward. She looked at him, and the agitation building up inside her chest disappeared. She smiled. "Thank you, dear."

"Just so you know I haven't forgotten how to be a gentleman." He gave her a toothy grin.

"You were always that, Cal," she murmured.

He settled in, steering the table a little away from him. "Let's not fight, honey. I shouldn't have made that crack about the kids. They can do whatever makes them happy." He gave her another grin. "Guy has to count himself lucky with a wife like you, and I always have."

"That's very sweet of you to say, dear."

A voice cleared beside them, and the waiter tactfully put the menus on the table and withdrew. Calvin mumbled to himself, "Can't understand what half this stuff is." He leaned forward, squinting through his glasses. "Chicken Marengo? What in the world is that?"

"'Chicken garnished with crawfish and fried egg,'" Leanne said. "It says so right there."

"Menus are like contracts these days," he said ruefully to the waiter. "You have to read the fine print. Good thing my wife does that for me."

Leanne's gut tightened when she heard the words "my wife". He always sounded territorial when he spoke of her to others, like a homesteader staking his claim. But her voice was pleasant enough as she ordered the Chicken Marengo.

"I'll have the same," he said. "You want wine, don't you?" He glanced at her. "We can't make a toast without it."

"Cal, I really think —"

"It's my wife's birthday." He winked at the waiter. "I won't tell you how old she is. She might get mad!" He roared with laughter. The waiter smiled with the same tact he had shown earlier as he congratulated her.

When he was gone, she searched her mind for something safe she could say to Calvin. "Who recommended this place?"

"Pauly," he said. "No one else I know would send us to this kind of hoity-toity spot."

"Paul is almost thirty with a wife and child, Cal," she said carefully. "I don't think it's appropriate to call him by a little boy's name." She examined the silver knife. "Not to mention, his knowledge of Impressionist art is as good as any sophisticated collector."

"Paul's a good fellow," Calvin agreed.

"You say that because he's always volunteering to do the work you loath," she remarked, smiling a little.

"There are some things beneath the position of a professor," he said stiffly. "That's why we have assistants."

"If you think so highly of him, why haven't you ever invited him and Arlene for dinner?"

"I explained it to you once," Calvin said.

"But you're his graduate advisor and graduate advisors don't get involved in their students' lives," she repeated. "I've seen some of the faculty treat their graduate students like sons and daughters."

Calvin shrank back. "That's not my way, Leanne. I take precautions to keep some distance from my students." He then proceeded to explain to her, his mustache quivering with pride, his elaborate method of "keeping distance" from his students.

"But you just admitted Paul is different from other graduate students."

"I never said anything like that." His thick fingers began to wander to the center of the table, examining the salt and pepper shakers, the card that told of the weekly specials, the toothpick holder. "I said he's a good fellow."

"You're taking restaurant recommendations from him, aren't you?" she pointed out. "That's a high compliment, coming from you."

"I take restaurant recommendations from anyone I know," he countered.

"Well, not for this kind of fancy restaurant. So you must trust him better than just one of your students benefiting from your engineering expertise."

"I *am* an expert in my field," he said, a little hurt.

"I wasn't suggesting you weren't, dear." She ran her finger against the cold film on her water glass. This seemed to finish the conversation and they sat silent for a while.

He cleared his throat. "You like this place?"

She nodded. "Just the kind of restaurant I would expect Paul to recommend."

"He's going to get too big for his britches one of these days," Calvin snorted.

"Why?" she asked. "Because he has an artistic nature?"

Calvin laughed as the waiter brought their salads. "Well, if he does, he's never given any indication of it to me!"

"No, he wouldn't." Leanne picked up her fork. "Not to you."

"Better I'm his advisor than Wallaby or Meeths," he said. "They'd probably waste their time going to art exhibitions and galleries with him. That's not what Paul needs, not if he's going to be a good engineer."

Leanne could hardly hide her smile. "And you know just what he needs, don't you, dear?"

"Certainly," he declared.

The vinegar from the salad dressing burned her throat. The idea of Calvin, with his egg-like head, sitting on couch with his feet up on the coffee table, his hands folded over his bloated stomach, lecturing Paul about what he needed struck her as preposterous. Calvin, who spent his free hours squinting over crossword puzzles, reprimanding her on how she arranged her kitchen although he had never so much as made a cup of coffee in it, who could wear down an argument faster than the entire high school debate team. Calvin, the frightened little boy with the bloated man's stomach.

"Paul has good taste," she murmured as she finished the salad.

"Turns out he knows a lot about the restaurants around here," said Calvin. "The best ribs, the best burgers, the best roast chicken. And the cheapest, too." He looked down at the steaming plate the waiter placed in front of him with the Chicken Marengo neatly arranged over herb-speckled rice and sticks of asparagus in hollandaise sauce.

She smiled. "He knows a lot about Impressionism too."

"What?" Calvin asked with his mouth full.

"An artistic movement from the nineteenth century," she said. "I explained it to you once. Several times, in fact."

"I don't have time for hoity-toity stuff," he grumbled.

"I was telling you something about your lab assistant!"

He took the handkerchief out of his pocket and loudly blew

his nose so that the couple sitting next to them glared. "Too much pepper for my taste."

"I think it's just perfect," she said. "He's studied the Impressionists. He even went to Paris and saw Monet's studio."

"All young men get funny ideas before they settle down to a nice, sturdy career." Calvin called the waiter over. "More water, please. This is a little spicy for my taste."

"Sorry, sir," the young man mumbled as he withdrew.

"He wants to be an art collector," Leanne continued. "He has a small collection already." She sat still for a moment. "I saw it this afternoon."

Calvin's balding head reflected red spots under the chandelier lights, and his cold green eyes sliced through the red and white room. "That may be, but I think Paul's too sensible to throw his life away trying to make his hobby a profession. I know him better than you, after all."

"I don't see that his desire to be a collector has anything to do with his career as an engineer," she pointed out. "The two don't have to be mutually exclusive."

"That's how much you know about the engineering profession." He picked up a roll. "I'm sure Arlene won't stand for this art collecting nonsense. Now, there's a prudent young woman. Not like these flighty, flouncing types who go around with these puffed-up hairdos and their skirts above their knees."

"She's also a biologist." Leanne eyed him. "I thought you didn't approve of women going into the sciences."

He scoffed, "She won't be a biologist for long. After she gets her degree, she'll go back to where she belongs with her husband and son and let Paul do his duty." He picked up the wine glass. "Anyway, I thought you didn't like her."

"I never said that," she said quickly.

"You were making some pretty snippy remarks about her a few months ago after the faculty party."

"I know," she said softly. "It was mean-spirited of me."

He leaned back to allow the waiter to take away his plate. Pointing to her plate, he said, "My wife will take the rest of that home."

Leanne stared down at her half-eaten food, her eyes clouding in the bright room, the soft clinking of the china, and the murmur of pleasant voices.

"The Crème Brûlée is supposed to be really something here," Calvin said. "We haven't had that in a while. Maybe now that Linda is out of the house, you'll have time to go back and experiment in the kitchen."

"Like I have time to do nice things for the neighbors?" She glared. "You make too many assumptions, Cal."

"But you said you enjoyed the birthday party!"

She sank down into the chair. How could she explain to someone like Calvin that the discovery of Melpomene and Thalia had been the cause of her joy, not standing over a bunch of kids making sure they didn't drop ice cream on their clothes?

"You used to make a good Crème Brûlée when we were first married," she heard him grumble.

"When have I had the time for such things?" she snapped. "I had two children to take care of!"

"Well, don't bite my head off," he said. "It was only a suggestion."

"I'll thank you not to make any more 'suggestions' about how I should spend my time."

His mustache curved into a sulk. "If you'd rather waste your time on those cuckoo horoscopes and charts, that's up to you." His smile was laced with malice.

"My 'cuckoo' interests are as important to me as your lectures are to you!"

"I suppose you plan on becoming some spiritual guide like that kooky Amber," he snarled. "Her in her moo-moos and those bracelets of hers making a racket every time she moves."

"At least she's not selfish like your precious Paul!" Her voice was a low bark, though the tables around them were now empty.

"Paul selfish?" He laughed. "I told you, you don't know him."

"He used his wife's inheritance to buy art." She felt her stomach churn. "I suppose you approve of that?"

He blinked behind the owl glasses. "Well, couples should share everything, shouldn't they?"

The waiter appeared at that moment with a calm, inquisitive look. "Bring my wife the Crème Brûlée," Calvin mumbled.

"I don't want it!" In a more even tone, she said, "I'd like the caramel parfait, please."

"Make mine Crème Brûlée, then." Calvin thrust the dessert menus into the waiter's hands.

Leanne sensed the young man knew the evening was wearing thin on them, as when he brought the desserts, he also set down a plate with two scoops of vanilla ice cream and a pile of whipped cream, giving her a sympathetic smile. "Compliments of the house."

"Someone must have broken the bottle of chocolate syrup," said Calvin with his clownish grin. "Take it back, and bring us one without all that syrup."

"Do you always have to put everyone out?" Leanne snapped when the young man was gone.

"I'm the customer, aren't I?" Then, in a calmer tone, "Come on, honey. We said we wouldn't argue."

She sighed. "You're right. I don't know what's come over me."

"You've been idle since Linda left," he said. "I know that. With both the kids gone, the house must be pretty empty."

"It's not the house that's empty," she murmured. "It's me. I'm empty like a garbage truck that's just been taken to the dump."

"That's hardly a nice way to talk about yourself." He chuckled. "Hey, remember when we were first married, you brought home that turnip cabbage but you didn't have a clue what to do with it? I thought you made a pretty good vegetable soup."

She grimaced. "You keep talking like you want me to be another Julia Child."

"Oh, nothing like that," he insisted. "But you used to love cooking."

"I hate cooking." She looked at him squarely. "I've always hated it."

"You're a good cook," said Calvin. "The kids always thought so. I always thought so."

"I hate cooking," she repeated, her voice amplified in the dull air. The jellied parfait stuck in her throat like the muddled words of his old-fashioned slang.

"For heaven's sake, why?"

"Because it takes such a damn long time!"

"Don't use words like that, Leanne." He glanced around. "It's not nice for a woman to swear."

"All of it does," she continued in a softer tone. "Cooking, cleaning, laundry. It eats away the minutes so there's no space left for what really matters."

"And what 'really matters' to you?" He eyed her. "All those cuck — all that weird stuff you have in the corner of the den. Those books you read, and those charts you study with a magnifying glass?"

"Why not?" She let her fork drop on the plate. "Why not?"

"Well, now you'll have time for everything, won't you?" His seething smile appearing again. "You can even be a spiritual teacher like Amber." The last was said with a callous look.

The waiter again seemed to pick up on the tension between them and rushed to place the bill at the edge of the table. "You folks just take your time," he mumbled.

A smack of red caught Leanne's eye. She realized there was a large stamp across the bill total. It said PAID.

Calvin, however, took no notice as he carefully slid his wallet out of his pocket.

"It's been paid, sir," prompted the waiter.

"Can you take the tip out of this?" His face was moony as it peered at the young man, waving a bill at him.

Leanne recognized his waning attention, a sign that the day had worn on him. "He said the bill's been paid, Cal."

His empty, blinking eyes stared at her, then looked at the waiter. "By whom?"

The waiter gave him a nervous smile. "I'm afraid the party asked to remain anonymous."

"Is that common?" Calvin asked.

"What does it matter?" Leanne said. "It's been paid, it's been paid."

"I have to know these things," said her husband. "Well?" He peered at the waiter again.

The young man began clearing away the coffee and empty dessert plates. "Oh, sure. We get that all the time."

"Well, I'd like to know who did it." Calvin struggled to put his wallet back in his pocket. "Can't properly thank someone for paying your meal if you don't know who he is."

"Well, sir," said the waiter, "the party did ask us to tell Mrs. Stewart — is that you, ma'am?"

"Yes." She tensed.

"The Muses are out."

In the car driving home, Calvin immediately started in on her. "What's that message about?"

"I haven't the faintest idea," Leanne said. She stared straight ahead so he wouldn't see she was lying.

"This isn't that Amber's doing, is it?"

She gave him a rueful grin. "Amber is far too spiritual to think of such a thing."

"Well, I'll be — " Calvin's voice cracked in the quiet car. "I can't understand it. No one knew we were coming here."

"This isn't a police investigation, Cal." Leanne stared out the window at the dark street.

"Paul knew," her husband corrected. "He recommended the

place, after all. I guess he's the one who did it. Not that he could have known we'd go there. We talked about several places, so I might just as well have taken you somewhere else."

"I don't think it was Paul."

"Well, who then?" His eyes scrutinized the road. His vision, like his hearing, faltered at the end of the day.

"You wouldn't believe me if I told you," she said, thinking of Arlene. *The Muses are out.*

"I've got to buy him some kind of present now, don't I?" Calvin grumbled as he turned into the driveway. "Can't let him spend his hard-earned money like that." They made their way down the walk, damp from a light rain earlier in the evening. "A bottle of wine, do you think? A basket of fruit? Or is that too chintzy?"

Leanne sighed as she slipped off her coat. "Whatever you want, Cal."

"Oh, well, you think of something." He gave a big yawn. "It was a nice evening, anyway. Don't you think it was a nice evening?"

"It's been an enlightening day," she said vaguely.

"Coming to bed?"

"Not yet," she said. "Cal, I think you ought to know, I've made a decision." She faced him. "I'm going back to school."

"Think they'll let you in with all those little tykes?" He gave her a clown smile.

"I'm not joking," she said. "I mean it. I'm going back to college."

"You're going to follow Linda to Purdue?" He still had on the clown smile. "That's one way to beat the loneliness, isn't it? When the mountain can't come to Mohammed, Mohammed goes to the mountain, or something like that, right?" He undid his tie. "Come on, honey, I was only kidding about the Crème Brûlée. Of course, you should do whatever you want with your time now that the kids are out of the house. You earned it."

"I'm so glad you think so," she said with an ironic smile. "Because I intend to take courses at the Center of Spirit and Light in San Francisco."

The dim stairway kept her from seeing his expression, but she knew he was bewildered by the way his thick fingers suddenly stopped drumming on the banister. "Don't tell me you took me seriously! I was teasing you about that spiritual teacher business."

"You were teasing," she said. "I'm not. I told you, Cal, I'm empty right now, and I want to replace that emptiness with something that really matters to me."

"You have something that matters!" he insisted. "Haven't I given you a home? Haven't you had a husband and two children to take care of? Doesn't all that matter?"

She felt stung inside. "Of course it does. I never said it didn't. But I'd like other things to matter too."

His face became stiff, the flabby features drawn. She knew he was going into one of his ornery moods. "I won't have my wife going around in moo-moos and reading the stars. You're an engineer's wife and you should act like it."

In a calm, unwavering voice, she said, "I'm going to do this, Cal. I'm not asking for your permission or your approval. I'll get some kind of job to pay for the courses."

He blinked. "What could you do, Leanne?"

"I can do plenty," she said. "I used to work in the college cafe before we were married. You didn't know that, did you?"

His face deflated like a balloon. "No, I never knew that."

"I intend to do this, with or without your help," she went on. Then, she turned to the living room. "I'll come up in a little while. I want to do some reading. Good night, Cal."

"Well, morning's the time for talking." He shrugged. "Don't make any decisions now. We'll talk about it in the morning."

Leanne knew that trick. He delayed things to "talk about in the morning" and then wrangled out of talking about them for days, hoping they would be forgotten and he wouldn't have to face them. She realized she was at fault too, because she usually did let them slide away like sand under waves.

"All right, Cal," she said. "We'll talk about it in the morning."

She wandered into the den, a small, dark place Calvin had coveted almost the moment they moved into the house. The large desk in the corner was piled high with papers in a system that only made sense to him. The bookshelf was packed with hardcover books, most of them from Calvin's past courses. He never allowed her to throw out or give anything away, even though some of those books were from before the war. She knelt down and took the encyclopedia volume M-P and sat in the worn leather chair to look up the Muses. She read about Melpomene and Thalia and their seven sisters, imagining their graceful presence floating around the room like strands in a breeze.

She didn't realize she had dozed off until the piercing sound of a bell startled her awake. She grabbed the phone off the desk.

"Happy Birthday, Mom!" The buoyant voice at the other end still had the honey tones Leanne remembered in the five-year-old Linda, though her daughter was now almost twenty.

"Darling, you shouldn't be up so late."

"I had to call and wish my mother a happy birthday, didn't I?"

"You could have called tomorrow morning," she said.

"What good is it to wish someone a happy birthday the day after?"

"It's called a belated birthday wish." Leanne laughed.

"Well, now you can tell all your friends your daughter didn't forget your birthday," said Linda. "Did Bill call?"

"No," said Leanne.

"Oh, well, don't be hurt. He's like Dad, you know. Sort of gets wrapped up in himself."

Leanne eased into the chair, feeling its comforting arms on either side. "How are things at Purdue?"

"Grand!" her daughter said. "I adore all the technical talk."

"I hope the young men in the class appreciate your enthusi-asm," said Leanne.

"Oh, there are two other girls," she said. "I don't think the boys even notice us. They're much too busy learning about thermal effects and structural problems on reentry!"

Leanne laughed. "It sounds like you've found Urania."

"Who?"

"Oh, one of the nine Muses in Greek mythology," said Leanne. "She was the muse of the heavens and the stars."

"Sounds like she's more your muse than mine," her daughter said.

"She's both our muse, then," Leanne said.

"I didn't know you knew about Greek mythology."

"I'm going to know a lot more things in the future."

"Good!" her daughter screeched. "It's about time Dad wasn't the only one who went in for higher learning."

"Your dad is tied to his logical arguments," said Leanne. "But we women, we walk with the Muses."

"Why, that's nice, Mom," said Linda. "I'm going to remember that."

When Leanne finally went to bed, she lingered at the window that looked on to the front street. Inside the folds of the velvet black sky, she could see a pattern of stars that took the shape of three slim women dancing in the forest in bright, flowing robes. She felt at peace with herself for the first time in twenty years.

Later that day, after her mother returned from the undertakers, she and Vivian retreated to the study to answer more condolences. The weight of melancholy returned as Vivian sat on the couch with telegrams and notes spread around her. Grandfather wandered in and, although Larissa spoke to him, he seemed not to hear her. He stared at the drawn curtains shadowing the pleasant peach and white hues.

She and her mother went on with their work with only the scraping of unfolding paper and the scrape of the fountain pen echoing in the quiet room with an occasional cough from Grandfather.

"The Taylors wrote us a very nice note, Father." Larissa held up a card.

"Yes, what?" He gaped at her.

"The Taylors, darling." Her mother's voice rose a few notches. "We were just talking about them last night. Do you want me to order you some coffee?"

His fingers gathered as if he were holding a cup and saucer in his hands, his eyes narrowing. Larissa reached for the bell cord.

"I don't think we should tell people the chapel is haunted,"

Vivian remarked as she tore open another envelope. "The Washington blue bloods are as superstitious as anybody."

"There is nothing to tell because it's not haunted," her mother insisted.

"Vixen in the dust, vixen in the dust," Grandfather threw his head back as if he were going to laugh. But no sound came out.

"Perhaps Grandmother had the chapel built to protect us from bad omens," Vivian said.

Her mother was no longer listening. She was reading a note, and her face, previously impassive with the business of correspondence, grew pallid.

"What is it?" Vivian peered at her.

She threw the note on the table. "What impertinence! What gall!"

The paper was as rough and plain as the envelope. There was no family emblem and no heading. The writing was neither light-handed nor curvy like other condolences Vivian had been reading. "It isn't from one of our friends, is it?"

"Certainly not!"

"Who is it from, then?"

"See for yourself." Larissa reached for the coffee pot Basset had brought in.

Vivian read:

Dear Mrs. Alderdice,

You don't know me though I feel as if you ought to. I was your mother's friend here in Waxwood. Indeed, oh, indeed, our fathers grew up together. Your mother and I were debutantes together, and Grace even gave me a picture for my 20th birthday, oh, it was very sweet and a little forlorn — but no matter.

I cannot express how heartbroken I was when I heard she was dead. Oh, how one forgets the years of one's youth, yes, one forgets. Or one puts them away like locks of hair from a beloved one knows will never return.

What must you think of me! I go off here and there now that I am old. My daughter Ruthie, she has such patience with me. Waxwood is the sort of place where one may lose one's measure. One may even lose oneself in an adventure! Grace certainly did. But she was never really lost, was she, for she had me and Mama and Papa and Loretta and oh, so many of us who loved her. No, indeed, she was not lost. She was only misplaced. Or is that losing oneself as well? Well, no matter.

I read the funeral is invitation only, but you will allow us to come to the funeral, I'm sure. Grace and I were such good friends. Surely, a fine lady such as yourself would not deny an old woman who goes off now and then that last sanction.

Remind me to your father.

Bertha Ross

"An odd letter," Vivian murmured.

"Odd is putting it mildly, dear. It's a crank, a hoax of some sort." Larissa slid the sugar bowl back on the tray. "One is apt to encounter such people when there is a death in the family."

"You don't know who she is, then?"

Her mother leaned sideways a little so her ankles peered out from under the skirt of her dress. They were well covered, but their angularity strained the leather casing of the shoes she wore. Vivian recognized the sign. Her mother was trying to reestablish her equilibrium. "I've never heard the name before."

"Grandfather?" Vivian peered at him.

"Leave him alone!" The order cut into the darkened room.

"Why does she call Grandmother 'Grace'?" she asked.

"Because she's mad," her mother insisted.

"No," Vivian said. "No, I believe she's sincere." She placed the note on the table.

Larissa grimaced. "Fools are always sincere."

"Where is Waxwood?"

"Stop asking so many questions, Vivian." Her mother reached for her fountain pen. "We can't have her coming to the funeral."

"Bad luck, bad luck," Grandfather murmured.

"It certainly is, Father," Larissa said. "Bad luck to have a madwoman at a funeral."

Vivian eyed her. "Superstition can't touch the Alderdices, remember?"

"Please, dear." Larissa's steady tone held a cutting edge.

Vivian watched as her mother leaned forward and scribbled a brief note. She pulled the bell cord. When Basset appeared, she thrust it at him. "Please send someone to deliver this as soon as possible."

"No reply, ma'am?"

"No reply."

When he was gone, Vivian said, "You're in rather a hurry to answer her, aren't you, Mother?"

"The funeral *is* tomorrow." Larissa gathered the rest of the envelopes. "She must not come."

Vivian felt her pulse rise. "It's rather cruel of you to refuse this poor woman the right to pay her last respects."

"I told you, dear, it's all a hoax. A terrible hoax!"

Vivian had never seen her mother so nervous. Her forehead was damp, and her shoulders looked as if they had frozen into a shrug. "What harm could there be in her coming?" she asked.

"Bad luck, bad luck!" Grandfather was off again, his hand in sword position.

"Don't upset yourself, Father," said Larissa.

"Perhaps it would be bad luck," Vivian said. "But not because she's a madwoman or a fool."

Her mother rose. "See that you finish your duties, Vivian." She placed the rest of the unopened envelopes on the couch. "And send for Basset to see to your grandfather, will you, dear? I believe he's quite tired."

When Larissa had left the room, Vivian looked at him. "Do you know who Bertha Ross is, Grandfather?"

He had gone bewildered again, but Vivian saw his eyes were alert.

Her mother had left Bertha Ross' note lying on the table. Vivian placed it back in its envelope, folded it, and slipped it up her sleeve.

Intrigued? Start your journey through the Alderdice family saga for FREE by following this link: https://tammayauthor. com/books-2/waxwood-series/the-specter-waxwood-series-book-1

How about that cool freebie I promised you? If you're into historical cozy mysteries featuring strong women who don't let society's rules about female behavior stop them from doing what they want, I urge you to check out the Adele Gossling Mysteries! Read on for how to get hold of the series' free novella, *The Missing Ruby Necklace*.

When a jewel and a girl go missing on New Year's Eve...

Eleanor McCarthy, a lovely though somewhat flighty debutante, has graced the tiny town of Arrojo, California, with her presence. One of Arrojo's prominent ladies throws a New Year's Eve shindig to introduce her to Arrojo's high society — whatever little of it there is. Naturally, the daughter and son of one of San

Francisco's influential lawyers, Adele and Jackson Gossling, are invited.

But screa s replace popping champagne corks when Eleanor's priceless ruby necklace is discovered missing. And soon, so is Eleanor!

In this historical cozy mystery set in the early 20th century, follow Adele Gossling, stationary store owner and amateur sleuth, and her clairvoyant sidekick Nin Branch as they search for a ruby necklace that may or may not have been stolen and a young woman who may or may not have run away.

Want to read an excerpt from this book? I got you covered! Turn the page.

"Coffee!" Miss McCarthy laughed. "Heavens, no! I haven't had my first taste of champagne yet." She flung her hand out to her brother. "Bring me a bottle of champagne, my good man."

"I don't mind," he said.

Before he could saunter out the door, Mrs. Abberton jumped up. "I'll get it."

"I really think we ought to get coffee," Mr. Abberton mumbled.

"She wants champagne," Mrs. Abberton was almost stern. "It's a celebration, after all!" She practically fled from the room.

Adele followed her and caught her arm. She spoke in a soft tone. "Mrs. Abberton, why did Miss McCarthy faint?"

"She just told you, didn't she?" The woman gave a shrill laugh. "Albert said we ought to open some windows, but it was such a windy night, I —"

"It wasn't the windows," said Adele. "Or the corset."

"Of course it was!" The woman examined some bottles on the floor. "I never could read these labels."

"You were staring at Miss McCarthy as if something that wasn't there."

"What an imagination you have, dear." The woman said.

"Miss McCarthy had her hands on her throat when she fell," Adele continued. "You kept looking at her throat."

"Nonsense," the woman hissed.

"Miss McCarthy wasn't wearing her ruby necklace," Adele declared.

Mrs. Abberton tore through a row of bottles lying on a table. One rolled onto the floor with a crack and the bubbly drink spilled across the marble. She sunk into one of the chairs. "You're too observant, Miss Gossling."

"You saw it too."

"Just before the lights went out," she said. "But Eleanor is one of those girls who gets easily flustered with her jewelry. She says it weighs her down."

"If that's true, why were you so alarmed just now?" Adele said.

"I wasn't," the woman insisted. "She locks that necklace in a box. Albert tried to persuade her to put it in our safe at the finance company, but she refused."

"That's rather unusual," Adele said.

"Eleanor's a lovely girl, but rather flighty," The woman said in a harsh tone. "I expect Celestine spoils her."

"If the necklace is missing, there might be a theft involved," Adele suggested.

Jewelry goes missing all the time. But does that mean theft? And why is Mrs. Abberton so nervous?

How can you get your hands on a copy of *The Missing Ruby Necklace*, not available in any bookstore? Simple. Go to this link: https://landing.mailerlite.com/webforms/landing/12u0c3. What else will you get when you get this novella? How about fun facts about women in history and true crime classic mysteries, which are just as fascinating, if not more so, as contemporary true crimes?

ABOUT THE AUTHOR

Writing has been Tam May's voice since the age of fourteen. She writes stories set in the past that feature sassy and sensitive women characters. Her fiction gives readers a sense of justice for women, both the living and the dead. Tam's stories are set mostly around the Bay Area because she adores sourdough bread, Ghirardelli chocolate, and San Francisco history.

Tam is the author of the Adele Gossling Mysteries which take place in the early 20th century and features suffragist and epistolary expert Adele Gossling whose talent for solving crimes doesn't sit well with the town's more conventional ideas about women's place.

Tam has also written historical fiction about women breaking loose from the social and psychological expectations of their era. She has a 4-book historical coming-of-age series set in the 1890s titled the Waxwood Series and a post-World War II short story collection available.

Although Tam left her heart in San Francisco, she lives in the Midwest because it's cheaper. When she's not writing, she's devouring everything classic (books, films, art, music) and concocting yummy vegan dishes.

Tam May can be reached at:
WEBSITE: http://tammayauthor.com/
EMAIL: tammay70@tammayauthor.com
FACEBOOK: https://www.facebook.com/tammayauthor
INSTAGRAM: https://www.instagram.com/tammayauthor/
PINTEREST: https://www.pinterest.com/tammayauthor/

www.ingramcontent.com/pod-product-compliance
Lightning Source LLC
Chambersburg PA
CBHW031305120726
47906CB00003B/897